Praise for
Fortune's Journey

"A high-spirited historical adventure from one of today's best-loved writers. Careful research, enlivened by Bruce Coville's trademark humor and humanity, offers an unusual look at a lesser-known aspect of the westward expansion as well as displaying this author's extraordinary versatility."

—Curriculum Administrator

"Packed with Gold Rush action, this new novel by Bruce Coville is thoroughly satisfying."

—The Children's Book Quarterly

"A great historical romance set in the gold rush era. Young people will enjoy tagging along on *Fortune's Journey.*"

—VOYA

★ A Junior Library Guild Selection

In the untamed West anything could happen— and often did . . .

Two days later a ferryman took their wagon across the Missouri River into Kansas. When they finally stood on the far bank of the river, Fortune had a sense that they had left their old world behind them and were truly facing the great unknown.

The wagons assembled.

"Wagons West!" came the call.

The real journey has begun, thought Fortune.

Her thoughts were interrupted by a lurch and a thump, followed by a terrible cracking sound.

"We've broken an axle," said Jamie. His face was grim.

Watching the way Jamie took charge, Fortune almost wished he had been with them from the start. She quickly chased the thought from her mind. Fortune didn't want any help. The troupe was hers and she would lead it in her own way!

FORTUNE'S JOURNEY

Bruce Coville

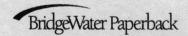

BridgeWater Paperback

Published by BridgeWater Paperback,
an imprint and trademark of Troll Communications L.L.C.

First published in hardcover by BridgeWater Books.

First paperback edition published 1997.

Printed in the United States of America.

10 9 8 7 6 5 4 3 2 1

Library of Congress Cataloging-in-Publication Data

Coville, Bruce.
Fortune's Journey / by Bruce Coville.
p.   cm.
Summary: Sixteen-year-old Fortune Plunkett faces many challenges on an
overland journey to California in 1853 with the acting company that she
inherited from her father.
ISBN 0-8167-3650-2 (lib. bdg.) ISBN 0-8167-3651-0 (pbk.)
[1.Theater—Fiction. 2. Overland journeys to the Pacific—Fiction.
3. Orphans—Fiction.] I. Title.
PZ7.C8344For   1995   [Fic]—dc20   94-38121

To Alice Morigi,
who insisted that I make it better, and helped me do so
with her wise and detailed comments. Whatever flaws
this story has now, they would be far greater without
the help of this grand lady of the theater.

CHAPTER ONE

Ahead lay San Francisco, and all their golden dreams. But that was more than half a continent away. All the six members of Plunkett's Players could see now, in the mid-afternoon of April 3, 1853, was the dreary road to Busted Heights, Missouri.

Fortune Plunkett, the group's leader, braced herself against the bumping of their gaudily painted wagon. The troupe had been traveling since sunrise, and there wasn't a bone in her body that didn't ache from the jouncing and rattling.

Even more annoying than the jouncing was the fact that she had been sitting next to Aaron Masters all day long, and he had virtually ignored her for that entire time. As she glanced up at him now, one of the wagon's wheels thudded into a mud hole. The wagon lurched sideways

"I hope we won't have to stay in a barn again," he continued now. "It's undignified!"

"That barn was dry," replied Fortune tartly. "And it was certainly better than the stable you were living in when we found you!"

"A temporary arrangement, I assure you. I would have been out of there in another day or so." Edmund's voice carried not the slightest hint that he didn't absolutely believe what he was saying. But then, he was an actor by trade.

Fortune sighed. The hiring of Edmund Wallach seemed to prove her father's oft-made claim that Henry Patchett was too softhearted for his own good. (Actually, Fortune's mother had often made the same claim about John Plunkett himself.)

The enormous man sitting next to Edmund scratched his gray beard and asked, "But how much farther *is* it?"

"Busted Heights, five miles," said Aaron, pointing to a wooden sign at the side of the road.

"If you would keep your eyes open, you wouldn't have to ask foolish questions, Walter," said Mrs. Watson, their leading lady. She smiled sweetly and adjusted one of the mother-of-pearl combs that held her long red hair in place.

"Sorry, Amanda," said Walter, ignoring the fact that he could not possibly have seen the sign from inside the wagon. He scratched his beard again, then lifted his derby and scratched the back of his head as well. Walter made it a point never to argue with Mrs. Watson. He had told Fortune it wasn't worth the effort, since she never listened to a thing anyone said.

"What's so important about this town that we had to go twenty miles out of our way to play it anyway?" asked Edmund querulously.

Fortune ignored the question. The trip to Busted Heights was something her father had insisted on. But he had not been willing to tell her why, saying only that he had something important to do in the town. "Unfinished business, Fortune. Unfinished business," was all he'd say whenever she asked about it.

Now he was gone, and though Fortune didn't know what the business was, she had decided to go through the town anyway. She figured if the "business" was important enough, it would find her.

When they reached the town an hour later, Fortune almost told Aaron to keep rolling. Busted Heights, population 407, was the most dismal spot they had landed in yet. It seemed the farther west they traveled, the more unpleasant the surroundings became. She hoped the trend wouldn't continue indefinitely.

13

As they rattled to a stop, Fortune found herself longing once more for the gracious sophistication of Charleston and the cozy house where she and her parents had lived when they were not traveling with a show.

If the other actors felt the same way, they didn't show it. Despite the unpaved streets and gray buildings of Busted Heights, they exploded from the wagon like bees from a toppled hive.

"Oh, lordy, that does feel good," said Mr. Patchett, stretching his long legs. "Today's ride was longer than an amateur production of *King Lear*!"

Fortune looked at him fondly. Tall—though not as tall as Walter—slender and beak-nosed, Henry Patchett had been her father's best friend since long before she was born.

"Get my bag, Walter," ordered Mrs. Watson.

"Certainly, my dear," replied the giant in a mild voice.

Fortune frowned. She didn't like the way Mrs. Watson treated Walter—or any of the rest of them, for that matter. Ever since the death of Fortune's mother nearly two years earlier, Amanda Watson had been trying to take on the role of Grand Lady for the troupe.

"Leave the bag," said Fortune, braving Mrs. Watson's scowl. "We've got a lot to do before dark. Let's get busy."

Familiar with the routine, they separated to tackle their jobs—Edmund and Aaron to put up posters announcing the troupe was in town; Mr. Patchett and Walter to find a space to perform in; Mrs. Watson to begin attracting men, which she did with remarkable skill.

As leader of the troupe, Fortune was responsible for finding their lodgings.

It didn't take her long to locate a likely looking boardinghouse—which for their purposes was one that didn't look as if it would charge much money. Tugging her dress slightly askew, Fortune reached up and pulled a wisp of her golden hair out of place. The moves were calculated to add to her waiflike appearance. Sometimes they helped, sometimes not. The fact that she was only five feet tall also helped, though most of the time she found her height—or lack thereof—wildly annoying.

Taking a deep breath, Fortune marched up to the door of the boardinghouse and knocked. She looked the place over while she waited. It was not very attractive. *Ugly would be a better word,* she told herself, trying to keep to her latest resolution of speaking her mind, even when it was only to herself.

The woman who answered the door was lean and bitter looking. She seemed, somehow, to fit the house. Her name, according to the sign out front, was Myra Halleck.

"I'd like to rent two rooms," said Fortune.

The Halleck woman looked at her suspiciously. "I only see one of you. What do you need two rooms for?"

She's the unfriendliest one yet, thought Fortune, bracing herself. Out loud, in what she hoped were her most innocent tones, she said, "There are six of us."

"Family?"

"Sort of."

The woman's pinched face took on a familiar scowl. "What's *that* supposed to mean?"

"We work together," said Fortune. "We're traveling players."

"Actors?" shrieked the woman. "In my house?"

Fortune winced. No matter how often she heard that tone of righteous indignation, she could never get used to it.

Papa, I can't do this, she thought. *I need you back.*

But John Plunkett wasn't coming back, so there was no point in thinking about it. Drawing herself up, Fortune said in a prim voice, "We are world-renowned thespians."

Her hope that the big word would put the woman off her guard was in vain.

"You may call yourself *thespians*," said the woman bitterly, fairly spitting the word. "*I* call you *frivolators.*"

16

Fortune gazed up at Mrs. Halleck and allowed two tears to form in the corners of her eyes. They trembled for a moment at the edge of her lashes, then spilled down her cheeks. "We do *good* shows," she said, letting a slight quaver creep into her voice. "You could bring your minister without any shame at all."

Mrs. Halleck stared at her for a minute, then relented. "All right, you can rent two rooms. But the rules are strict—and it will have to be money in advance!"

Fortune dug in her heels and started to negotiate. It wasn't long before she realized her little performance had been wasted. Once the old fraud had scented money, there was no chance of her turning them away. She had simply been setting herself up to charge as much as she could.

An hour later, pleased but not delighted by the deal she had worked out with Mrs. Halleck, Fortune went looking for the rest of her troupe. It wasn't hard to find them—the Conestoga wagon they were traveling in had been painted in brilliant colors. Tall scarlet letters on the canvas read PLUNKETT'S PLAYERS—AMERICA'S FINEST TRAVELING THEATRICAL COMPANY.

She had just spotted the wagon—as usual, it had attracted a handful of small boys—when Mr.

Patchett came striding toward her. Fortune smiled. With his prominent nose and long skinny legs, Henry sometimes made her think of a stork.

"Good news, Fortune! There's an empty room available above MacKenzie's General Store." He pointed to a wooden building across the street. "It's a good size. They even have dances in it sometimes. We open there tomorrow night with *The Widow's Daughter*."

Walter had come lumbering up beside them. He grimaced at the mention of the play. "When are we going to do some good shows again, Fortune?" he asked, staring mournfully down at her. "You know, the kind of thing your father—" He caught himself and started again. "The kind of thing we started out to produce."

"There's nothing wrong with *The Widow's Daughter*!" snapped Mr. Patchett. "The problem is with you, Walter. You're as stuck up as a kite in a tree."

Fortune sighed. The argument was as familiar, and as boring, as her worn blue dress. "We'll get back to those plays, Walter," she said, resting her hand on his arm. "I promise. Right now I've got one thing in mind, and that is to get us to California as Papa intended."

She turned and headed for the general store Mr. Patchett had indicated.

*　　*　　*

"You must be Miss Plunkett," said the heavyset man standing behind the counter.

"Guilty as charged," replied Fortune. "Are you Mr. MacKenzie? If so, then thank you for renting us your loft."

The man made a sound somewhere between a snort and a grunt. "It'll be good to have some entertainment around here," he said, straightening a row of tin containers that stood on the counter. "You folks find a place to stay yet?"

Fortune nodded. "We're at Mrs. Halleck's boardinghouse."

MacKenzie laughed. "I bet things are a little edgy around *there* about now."

"Why would that be?" asked Fortune innocently.

"The Widow Halleck doesn't much care for any kind of frivolity. In fact, I'd say the only thing she hates worse than actors is missing out on a chance to make a penny. So she's going to be feeling kind of funny about having you folks in the house; kind of like letting the devil through the front door, if you know what I mean."

Fortune nodded. She knew all too well how some people felt about actors—and actresses. She turned the conversation to the kind of fabric she was looking for. Mr. MacKenzie showed her where he stored the bolts of material, and soon Fortune

19

was lost in daydreaming. The homely goods—pots and pans, bolts of fabric, even the mop buckets—gave her a sharp stab of longing.

She wanted a home of her own!

She cut the thought off ruthlessly. For now, the wagon was her home. Besides, thoughts of home brought with them pictures of her parents. The wounds their deaths had sliced into her heart had not yet healed enough for Fortune to deal with them.

Forcing herself to look around, she spotted a bolt of calico cloth. It would make a lovely dress. Maybe if the take was good tomorrow night . . .

That was silly and she knew it. Even if the take *was* good, any extra money had to be reserved for the trip west. Even so, she ran her fingers along the fabric, planning out the lines of the dress. Turning the bolt over a few times to let out the cloth, she lifted a length of the fabric to her throat, then turned to the window, hoping to catch her reflection so she could see what the dress might look like played against her blue eyes and blond hair.

To her surprise, she saw someone watching her.

The face looking in at the window was young and pleasant, its owner lean and deeply tanned. He had a crooked smile, high cheekbones, and large brown eyes that would have come dangerously close to making him pretty if it had not been for a slight scar that cut through his right eyebrow. His unruly mop of chestnut brown hair appeared to resist any attempts to hold it in place.

When the boy realized Fortune was looking back at him, a blush fought its way through his tan. Averting his eyes, he stepped away from the window.

Fortune looked down at the calico. But from the corner of her eye she tried to keep track of her admirer. After a moment of indecision he stepped into the store.

He was taller than Fortune had realized, easily more than six feet. His shapeless cotton shirt did nothing to hide his broad shoulders and narrow hips. A slight curl of brown hair at the neck of the shirt completed the picture. Fortune realized with a start that he had what the ladies in Charleston had called "boyish charm"—and lots of it.

"Afternoon, Jamie," said Mr. MacKenzie with a slight nod. "What can I do for you?"

"I need fifty pounds of flour," said Jamie. He was looking sideways at Fortune, trying hard to pretend he didn't notice her.

"You must be planning on a lot of baking," said Fortune with a laugh. She realized she was in one of her teasing moods, something her father had always claimed was a bad thing for any innocent bystanders. She looked Jamie over, feeling very sophisticated. He was handsome, but such a bumpkin he probably had hayseeds in his hair.

Jamie was blushing again. "My mother feeds a lot of people."

"I imagine you must help her," said Fortune slyly. "You should make someone a wonderful husband."

Even the tips of Jamie's ears were crimson now. But instead of retreating, he clenched his jaw and looked directly into her eyes.

"I suppose I would," he said. "Are you interested?"

At once the color drained from his face. Tossing the sack of flour over his shoulder as if it weighed nothing, he rushed from the store in embarrassment.

"What's the matter with the lad?" asked Mr. Patchett, storking his way through the door. "He almost ran me down. He looked paler than Walter when he's made up to be the ghost of Hamlet's father!"

Fortune began to laugh. MacKenzie looked at her and lifted an eyebrow.

"I know, I know," she said. "That was cruel, and I shouldn't have done it. But he was just so . . . so . . ."

It was the storekeeper's turn to chuckle. "You can explain when you see him again," he said.

Fortune looked startled. "What do you mean?"

MacKenzie's smile grew broader. "That was Jamie Halleck. You're staying at his mother's house."

Fortune groaned. She had done it again!

CHAPTER TWO

Jamie Halleck placed a huge platter of fried chicken on the table. Casting a sidelong look at Fortune, he left the room.

Fortune felt herself flush.

Edmund laughed raucously, his dark eyes flashing. "Looks like you have an admirer, little Fortune."

Fortune's blush deepened. "My name is Fortune," she said tersely. "Plain Fortune."

Edmund smiled. "*He* doesn't think you're plain."

"Now, Edmund," clucked Mrs. Watson. "Leave the girl alone. Of course she has admirers. Why, when I was her age, the boys were flocking around me."

"Mrs. Watson!" said Aaron admiringly. "What a memory you have!"

The actress flared. "I remember that in my day young men had manners," she said imperiously.

"You'd better tend to them, Master Aaron, or young Fortune might start looking at that Jamie the way she looks at you."

Walter covered his laugh with a snort and tried to pretend it was a sneeze.

I'd like to crawl under the table and die, thought Fortune as her blush continued to deepen. She was deeply grateful when Mr. Patchett cleared his throat and loudly asked if everyone was ready for a rehearsal later that evening.

At once the troupe launched into a vigorous argument over the merits of *The Widow's Daughter,* the quality of their parts, and the stupidity of the anticipated audience. Fortune silently thanked Mr. Patchett for changing the subject.

Except for the fact that she was in an agony of embarrassment, the dinner was better than Fortune had expected. The Widow Halleck was such a fierce hawk of a woman it had seemed unlikely anything pleasant could come out of her kitchen Yet the chicken was tasty, the biscuits light and fluffy, the gravy smooth and savory.

She wondered if Jamie had really helped make them. She was also bothered by the knowledge that she herself could not do it half so well.

Jamie returned from the kitchen with another platter. The hungry group around the table fell upon it like vultures.

Fortune averted her eyes. When she had teased Jamie in the store, it had seemed unlikely she would have any close contact with him again. Except for the time the men spent in the saloons, Plunkett's Players lived pretty much to themselves when they were on the road. It hadn't occurred to her that the awkward young man would be their host here in Busted Heights. Mr. Patchett had been quite upset with her, too; he was anticipating enough trouble with their landlady as it was.

Indeed, even as Jamie disappeared back into the kitchen, they could hear the shrill voice of Mrs. Halleck complaining to the hired girl. "I don't know why I let those people in here. Actors? Tools of the devil is more like it. Frivolators, I call 'em—"

Then the door was closed and they could hear no more. Yet it almost seemed it had been left open longer than necessary. Fortune wondered if Jamie had hesitated on purpose, just to make sure the troupe could hear his mother's opinion of them.

She shrugged. What difference did it make? She certainly didn't care what Jamie Halleck *or* his mother thought of them.

She bit her lip. The problem was, she did care, and she knew it. Try as she might, she could never convince herself that the people who looked down on actors didn't matter.

Fortune swatted the thought away. She had no

time for such nonsense. They were going to rehearse after dinner, and she had to go over her lines. Muttering an "Excuse me," she pulled away from the table and headed upstairs for the room she shared with Mrs. Watson.

Closing the door to her room behind her, Fortune looked around and wondered again why her father had started them on this westward trek.

When she was honest with herself, she knew why. John Plunkett had always been a restless man. When the discovery of gold in California had been announced in 1849, he had ached to head for the goldfields—not to mine ore, but to mine the audiences he knew were gathering there.

Unfortunately for his wandering soul, Fortune's mother, Laura, would have nothing of it. But in June of 1851 Laura Plunkett had been struck down swiftly and silently by one of the thousand diseases that made life in the mid-1800s chancy at best.

With the loss of his wife John Plunkett had gone a little bit crazy. A year later, no longer tied down by Laura's need for a regular home, he had packed up his daughter and the rest of his acting troupe to join the westward trek.

Fortune had not argued; at the time she had been more than willing to leave Charleston, to flee the memories, happy and sad, that seemed to haunt her on those streets.

Thus the troupe had become Plunkett's *traveling* Players, and Fortune Plunkett had become a virtual gypsy. And as they traveled from town to town, moving ever westward, she had discovered that despite the hardships her father was right about one thing: Wherever there were people, there was a need for entertainment.

"The whole country is growing westward," he would tell Fortune. "And the ones who get there first are going to do the best."

These remarks were usually prompted by his reading some article about how San Francisco had become a booming city, eager for new experiences, for "culture" to come to its western wildness. When he read that the Chapman Family's performances were sometimes rewarded by miners flinging bags of gold dust onto the stage, their course was fixed. The city beckoned to him like a distant dream.

Fortune sighed. In the past her dreams and her father's had been in conflict. But with his death she had had to make his dreams her own.

She shook her head and forced herself out of her reverie. San Francisco might be a booming city, but right now she was in Busted Heights. She looked around again. The small room was clean enough, but that was about all that could be said for it. The walls were bare except for a cracked mirror hanging above a small stand that held a basin and pitcher for washing up. The lone bed, sagging in the middle, was scarcely wide enough for two. Sharing it with Mrs. Watson, who not only tossed and turned but tended to snore, was going to be an ordeal. A single, spindly chair provided the only other resting place. The one spot of brightness in the room was a beautiful handmade quilt that covered the bed. Fortune wondered if Mrs. Halleck had made it.

She picked up the quilt and examined it. The stitches were tiny and even. The pattern, one she did not recognize, was lively and intricate. It was hard to think of that harsh, angry woman doing such lovely work. But if Fortune had learned anything from her years in the theater, it was that people often had many sides.

Mrs. Watson, for example: She liked to present herself as a woman of the world—strong, independent, and sophisticated. Yet sometimes at night, when she thought Fortune was sleeping, she would cry quietly for hours at a time. And once Fortune had seen her throw a vase of flowers through a plate-glass window in reaction to a bad review.

Fortune put down the quilt and wandered to the window.

In the street below she saw Aaron leaning

against a fence post, talking to a pretty young girl. Fortune felt her hands tighten on the sill. Why did he look so interested in the stranger? And why did he persist in treating her, Fortune, like nothing but a kid sister?

"Men!" she said in disgust and turned back to the room. Opening the carpetbag that sat next to the door, she drew out the worn script she shared with Mrs. Watson and sat on the bed to review her lines for *The Widow's Daughter.*

After a moment she threw the script to the floor. She knew her lines perfectly well; they had done the play more times than she cared to remember, and she hated it more every time they performed it. It was a ridiculous story about a poor widow who was being hounded by two men who wanted to marry her daughter. One was rich and rotten, naturally; the other, poor but honest and upright.

Fortune played the daughter. Mrs. Watson had been playing her mother for the last year and a half, and to Fortune's dismay, she seemed to be taking the role to heart. Lately she had been trying to provide Fortune with more offstage mothering than she could stand.

Fortune also played three other roles in the play—the minister's wife, a farmer's son, and the town drunk. She wished they had some other actors. It was difficult to change parts so often. Sometimes she had to wear one costume under another so she could make her changes fast enough.

She sighed and got to her feet. Mr. Patchett would be ready to start soon, and she didn't want to keep him waiting. He had tried so hard since her father—

Fortune cut off the thought. Grabbing a shawl, she hurried down the stairs.

Mrs. Watson was waiting in front of the boardinghouse, talking with—or, more likely, *at*—a darkhaired little girl who was leaning against a post and staring up at her with wide and fascinated eyes.

"Ah, here you are," said Mrs. Watson when she spotted Fortune.

The child took her finger out of her mouth long enough to say, "You're pretty!" then popped it back between her lips again.

"So are you," said Fortune, kneeling in front of her. That wasn't entirely true; the child had a pinched, crabbed look that made Fortune suspect that she didn't get enough to eat. But it made the child smile.

"What's your name?" asked Fortune.

The girl shook her head.

"It's Nancy Conaway," said Mrs. Watson.

"You told!" said the girl accusingly.

Mrs. Watson gasped. "I forgot it was a secret!" she exclaimed, overacting as usual.

Nancy Conaway giggled, then went running down the street.

Mrs. Watson does make a good Mother Hen, thought Fortune. *Too bad she doesn't have about a dozen more chicks. Then she could spread her attention around a little and leave me alone.*

"I was waiting for you," said Mrs. Watson, taking Fortune's arm. "I thought we should walk over together. It's not good for us ladies to be out alone."

Several men stopped to stare admiringly at them as they walked across the rutted dirt road and then down to the general store. Fortune wasn't surprised. Mrs. Watson was extremely good looking for a woman in her thirties. And while the dress she was wearing, perfect for an afternoon tea in Charleston, was totally out of place in a dreary little town like Busted Heights, it was a real attention-grabber.

Aaron, looking smug and self-satisfied, was waiting for them at the general store. "It's about time you got here," he said. "Mr. Patchett's about to have kittens."

Mrs. Watson laughed. "Get along with you, Aaron. Here, take me up the stairs."

She extended an arm, which Aaron took with only the slightest show of reluctance. He was used to such requests.

Fortune followed them around the side of the store, where an outside stairway led to the second floor.

She was pleased with the playing space. The oil lamps that Walter and Mr. Patchett had lit revealed the loft to be spacious, with an unexpectedly high ceiling. Better yet, there were several windows to allow them some fresh air. Sometimes it got so stifling when they were acting! She noticed a makeshift stage at the far end of the room and guessed that they probably used it for the musicians when they had dances here.

Walter, Edmund, and Mr. Patchett were standing at the front of the room waiting for them. They had already carried up the trunk that held most of the properties they would need for the play. Mr. Patchett was tapping his foot and looking impatient.

As Fortune turned to finish her survey of the room, she became aware of one more person. Jamie Halleck was sitting in a chair against the side wall.

"What are *you* doing here?" she asked disapprovingly.

He looked startled by the tone in her voice. "I . . . I just wanted to listen. I asked Mr. Patchett if it was all right."

"Well, wait till tomorrow night and pay, like everyone else," she said sharply. She turned away from him and headed for the front of the loft.

"I had intended to," said Jamie coldly. Fortune stopped. His voice, which had seemed childish, almost afraid, was suddenly deep and masculine. She turned back toward him.

Before she could speak, he cut her off.

"You needn't put on such airs," he said icily. "You're not the first actress I ever saw. But I love the theater, and we don't get much of it here in Busted Heights."

Something about the way he said "the theater"—a sense of reverence tinged by longing—reminded her of her father.

"Don't be so hard on the boy, Fortune," said Mrs. Watson, stepping up beside her. She lowered her voice and added, "Besides, it never hurts to have a handsome young man around. It might even keep that scamp Aaron on his toes."

Giving Fortune a wink, she patted her shoulder, then turned away.

Fortune looked back toward the door. Jamie was on his way out. "Oh, all right—you can stay. But don't interrupt! And I expect you to buy that ticket tomorrow night!"

He turned back, and Fortune caught her breath at the radiant smile that wreathed his face.

"Can we get started, please?" she shouted, partly to cover her own confusion.

Walter, who acted as her stage manager, scratched his beard. "Sure thing, Miss Fortune." Raising his voice he bellowed, "Take your places, everyone!"

There was a muted grumbling and a moment of confusion as the troupe shuffled into place for Act One, Scene One of *The Widow's Daughter.* Fortune took her position stage right and waited for her first entrance, which was some fifteen minutes into the play. Walter barked out a direction, and they began.

Fortune found herself yawning as Mr. Patchett launched into his big opening speech. She had always thought it was twice as long as it should be. She looked around and spotted Jamie watching the play with rapt attention. She studied his face more closely than she had been able to this afternoon in the store. *He certainly is handsome,* she found herself thinking, almost against her will. *I wonder why he's so interested in theater? It seems funny for such a . . .*

"Fortune . . . *Fortune!*"

She came to with a start. She had missed her entrance! Feeling extremely foolish, she leaped to her feet and raced to her position. A snort of amusement from Jamie made her skin begin to color.

Determined to recover from the blunder and show Jamie what she could do, she threw herself into the scene, crying out in despair over her mother's distress and reacting with terror to the advances of the wicked landlord. She ended by flinging herself over Mrs. Watson's knees and breaking into hysterical sobs.

Her performance earned a burst of wild applause from Jamie. "Wonderful!" he cried. "That was *wonderful!*"

Aaron broke into laughter. "You're an easy target."

Fortune started to flare at the insult to her performance.

Jamie beat her to it. "What do you mean?" he asked sharply.

"That was a lot of things, but it was hardly wonderful. You ought to see a real show someday."

"I'd love to."

Again Fortune caught that sense of breathless appreciation in his voice. Then she realized what Aaron was saying. "Wait a minute," she said angrily. "We're not that bad."

"Well, we're not that good," said Aaron. "If we were, we wouldn't be playing a hick town like this."

"This isn't a hick town!" bristled Jamie. "Just because people here don't have everything you city people might, it doesn't mean we're stupid!"

"Can we begin Act Two?" asked Walter. "If we finish this rehearsal early, we can all get a good night's sleep. You're welcome to stay," he added, turning to Jamie. "But please don't interrupt anymore."

Jamie opened his mouth to protest, then thought better of it. "Thank you, sir," he said mildly.

They began the second act. Again Jamie watched with shining eyes. Fortune caught herself playing directly to him, then felt foolish about it. *Well, why not?* she asked herself. *An audience is an audience, after all. It's good practice.* But she also knew she was enjoying his wide-eyed reaction.

They got through the rest of the play without incident, Jamie applauding enthusiastically after each scene.

"I think that will do it for now," said Mr. Patchett when they finished the run-through. "We're all set for tomorrow night. Edmund and Aaron, I'll need you to help me prepare the stage in the afternoon."

"Ah, the stage," said Walter, plopping his derby onto his head. "Our home away from home." He looked around the loft with an expression of distaste. "Of course, home is getting a little shabby these days. Oh, well. The immortal bard tells us that all the world's a stage, and all the men and women merely players."

"Actors," said Aaron.

"What?"

"Actors, Walter. The line is from *As You Like It*, and it says 'actors,' not 'players.'"

"It does not," said Walter indignantly. He turned to Mr. Patchett for verification. "It's 'players'—right, Henry?"

"I think so," said Mr. Patchett, obviously not certain himself.

"Actors," said Aaron.

"It's 'players,'" said Jamie. He came striding forward, his face glowing with excitement.

CHAPTER THREE

Aaron looked at Jamie angrily. "Why don't you stay out of this? Besides, how would you know?"

"Because I know the speech. It goes:

> *"All the world's a stage,*
> *And all the men and women merely* players.
> *They have their exits and their entrances,*
> *And one man in his time plays many parts,*
> *His acts being seven ages. At first the infant,*
> *Mewling and puking in the nurse's arms."*

Jamie's voice was soaring, powerful in its range of tone and expression. Fortune and the others stared at him in astonishment. He seemed not to notice, caught up as he was in the beauty of Shakespeare's words. At the same time that Fortune wondered how he knew the speech, she found herself resisting another thought: The boy was good!

His voice dwindled with sorrow as he reached

the mournful concluding words:

"*. . . second childishness and mere oblivion,*
Sans teeth, sans eyes, sans taste, sans everything."

"Bravo!" cried Walter, obviously delighted both at being correct and at Jamie's masterful rendition of the lines.

Mr. Patchett looked at Jamie with new respect. "Where did you learn that?"

"My father taught me. He loved Shakespeare."

"I'm sure we're all impressed," said Aaron, causing a snicker from Edmund.

Jamie's jaw tightened, the muscles around his mouth clenching as though he were biting back an angry retort.

Leave him alone, Aaron! thought Fortune, to her own surprise.

Jamie looked around the room. "I'm sorry," he said with great dignity. "I'm intruding."

Without another word he walked away from the group and disappeared down the stairway.

"Oh, Minerva!" said Mrs. Watson to Aaron. "Now see what you've done?"

"Me?" cried Aaron, his voice full of wounded innocence.

Fortune ignored them. She was trying to tell herself she was relieved that the intruder was gone.

Yet she couldn't stop staring at the doorway.

*   *   *

The next night Fortune stood behind one of the curtains that Walter and Aaron had draped at the right and left sides of the stage to mask the actors when they were not performing. Mr. Patchett had arranged the action to ensure that she and Mrs. Watson could always exit to the right to make their costume changes, while the men would always exit to the left.

She glanced over at Mrs. Watson, who was "preparing her face" for her grand entrance. Her red hair tumbled over her shoulders in thick, glossy curls.

Almost against her will, Fortune felt a wave of affection for this woman who had tried so hard to look out for her over these last months. At least she meant well.

Turning back to the curtain, she gently pulled back an edge so that she could check the audience. She felt a flash of guilt for this breach of professional ethics, but not enough to stop her from doing it.

The oil lamps at the front of the stage had been lit. Walter, already in costume, stood at the front, selling tickets. The house was filling nicely; they would probably have close to a hundred people.

To Fortune's surprise, she saw little Nancy Conaway sitting toward the back, all scrubbed and polished.

41

As she continued to look around, she found herself wondering if Jamie had arrived yet. She told herself the curiosity was only because she felt sorry for him. After she had heard his mother screaming at him this afternoon, Fortune had decided the young man deserved whatever fun he could manage. Especially since part of what Mrs. Halleck had been screaming about had had to do with how she would tan his hide if he ever considered going to "that wicked play" this evening.

Fortune scowled at the memory. Mrs. Halleck's abusive screeching had been a horrible thing to listen to. And even though it had been so loud that neither she nor anyone else within a hundred yards could help but hear it, she had felt as if she was eavesdropping.

"Nervous, dear?" asked Mrs. Watson.

Fortune dropped the curtain. "Of course not. Why should I be?"

Mrs. Watson gave her a sly grin. "I always find it gives me butterflies when I have an admirer in the audience."

"What are you talking about?" asked Fortune, a little too casually.

"Jamie, of course."

"Oh, *him.*" She waved a hand. "I hardly think you could call him an admirer."

Mrs. Watson paused in the application of her

makeup. "You know, I think you're right."

"What do you mean?" asked Fortune. *This is ridiculous,* she said to herself. *I'm not in the least bit interested in him. So why should it bother me if he's not interested in me? Vanity. That's what it is. You're getting vain, Fortune Plunkett. You'd better watch out, or you'll end up like Mrs. Watson.*

"I'll tell you what it is with that boy," said Mrs. Watson. She gave her face one last dab of powder and turned to Fortune. "He's stagestruck! Don't ask me how it happened out here in West Nowhere, but that's what it is. He's got it bad."

The older woman shrugged. "Of course, you being an actress and all, he naturally looks up to you. But it's the stage he's really interested in. You're right, Fortune. He's not an admirer after all."

Fortune looked at Mrs. Watson suspiciously. Was she teasing? The hint of a smile lit her face, but Fortune couldn't tell if it was because she was joking, or because she was feeling smug for having diagnosed Jamie's condition.

"Well, that's a relief," she said, forcing a smile herself. "I was beginning to worry about the poor boy."

"Oh, I wouldn't worry about him. Any lad who looks like he does won't lack for female companionship. But he'll go crazy in this little town if he doesn't get rid of that hankering for 'the theater.'"

Mrs. Watson altered her voice on the last two words, doing a perfect imitation of Jamie's worshipful way of saying them. Fortune laughed in spite of herself.

Suddenly they were aware of a silence on the stage. "Oh, Minerva!" cried Mrs. Watson. "That's my entrance!"

The older woman rushed off, leaving Fortune alone with her thoughts. After a moment she reached for the edge of the curtain and again scanned the audience.

She spotted Jamie sitting in the third row, and wondered how he had gotten around his mother's objections to his coming here . . . or what price he would pay once the fierce old harridan discovered where he had been.

She narrowed her eyes. Jamie was sitting next to a girl. Had they come together?

What difference does it make if they did? she asked herself sternly. *I certainly don't care if he has a girlfriend!*

She looked the young lady over.

She's pretty—but not as pretty as I am.

She lowered the edge of the curtain in disgust. What had gotten into her? What did she care whether the girl he was sitting with was pretty or not? She had Aaron to think about.

Aaron! She could hear his voice onstage. If she wasn't careful she would be like Mrs. Watson and miss her entrance.

She went to the edge of the stage and waited for her cue.

"And where is the widow's daughter?" asked Walter in his oiliest tones.

Fortune smiled. Walter made a wonderful villain—which was strange, since he was about the sweetest man she knew.

"Here I am!" she cried gaily, doing a pirouette as she made her entrance.

Her arrival prompted a burst of applause. Women were scarce in this area—and pretty ones were even scarcer. The men appreciated her beauty, and she enjoyed their appreciation. Out of the corner of her eye she noticed Mrs. Watson looking disgruntled. There had been slightly less applause at *her* entrance.

At the end of the first act the audience surged out of the loft. Fortune, experienced at reading the mood of a crowd, could tell things were going well. She caught a certain contented buzz, mixed with an angry undertone that spoke of outrage at the villain's behavior. They were really involved in the play.

Unfortunately, she knew many of the men would take advantage of the break to go next door to the bar for a drink. Others had already been drinking out of pocket flasks they had brought with them. Fortune frowned. The drunks they had to cope with in almost every audience were one of the things that bothered her most about their travels.

"Knock knock?"

It was Walter, standing outside their curtain.

"Come in!" said Fortune.

Walter lifted the makeshift door and ducked to step into their space. He was wearing a broad smile. "A good house tonight, Fortune. We took in enough to cover what we paid Mrs. Halleck, get the horses shod, and still have a little to spare."

Fortune returned his smile. That *was* good news. The troupe's day-to-day funds had been getting dangerously low, and she had feared they would have to dip into the money she was saving for the price of the wagon train they were planning to join at Independence. A few good nights would help avoid that unpleasant possibility.

"Thank you, Walter. Take good care of it, now, won't you?"

He winked. "I've got it tucked away safe and sound. I just wanted to give you the good news."

Fortune watched him leave. She found herself smiling affectionately. Walter was an old bear, that was all there was to it. A big cuddly old bear.

Edmund was next at their "door." Fortune frowned. The newcomer had developed an annoying habit of coming to their dressing room between acts on almost any excuse, and she didn't like the way his dark eyes flicked over her at those times. Now those eyes were smoldering, and his thin lips were pulled tighter than usual.

"Aaron has stepped on my lines three times tonight, Miss Plunkett. I would appreciate it if you would speak to him after the performance!" He spun on his heel and stalked away.

Fortune opened her mouth, but nothing came out. When Mrs. Watson burst out laughing, Fortune turned on her and cried, "What's so funny?"

Mrs. Watson was holding her sides. "Oh, you can't take that young peacock seriously. He's such a vain little thing. Thinks he can act, too!"

"He can," said Fortune. "Otherwise I'd tell Mr. Patchett to get rid of him. Unfortunately, we need him."

"And he needs us just as much. My advice is to just ignore him when he gets like that. Do you think he'd leave us? Where's he going to go, for heaven's sake?"

"Ready for Act Two!" It was Mr. Patchett, hissing through their curtain.

"Yes," called Fortune. "We're set to go."

She sighed. Three of the four men in the troupe had found reason to cross the stage and speak to her during intermission. Why not Aaron?

The audience was obviously in a good mood as the second act began. They cheered as Fortune and Mrs. Watson made their entrances, and booed loudly at the appearance of Walter-the-villain.

Fortune felt a little nervous. Their mood was a trifle *too* good. She knew from past experiences that rowdy audiences like this could get out of hand.

Her fears were confirmed ten minutes later when two men in the front row took objection to Walter's latest, most wicked scheme.

"You can't do that!" cried one of them, his words slurred by liquor. "Why, that woman's too good for you!"

"Who do you think you are, anyway, trying to bust up them kids?" cried the other. He stood, weaving unsteadily.

His partner leaped up beside him. "Come on down here an' fight like a man."

"Yeah," said the second. "C'mere an' fight like a man, ya big sissy."

Fortune winced. It wasn't the first time this had happened during a show. But the more drunk the interrupters were, the harder it was to get things settled down.

Mr. Patchett was moving to the edge of the stage when the second of the two men clambered up onto it. Lunging past Mr. Patchett, he grabbed for Walter. "C'mere, you weasel! I wanna teach you a lesson!"

Walter stepped aside. It did no good. The man stumbled after him. "C'mere, I said!"

Reaching up to grab Walter's shoulder, he gave it a fierce yank. Walter turned, raising an enormous arm to ward off the man's fist.

That was all it took to send the drunk sprawling to the floor. His outstretched arm struck one of the oil lanterns that lined the edge of the stage. It rolled off, cracked, and spilled oil across the floor.

The still burning wick touched off the oil spill. Flames raced along the oil, creating a low wall of fire across the front of the stage.

Cries of terror erupted from the audience. As a mass they leaped up and began scrambling for the doors.

Fortune grabbed Mrs. Watson's arm. "We've got to get out!" she cried. "Let's go!"

At that moment the blaze jumped to the curtain strung on the men's side of the stage. In a flash the fabric was engulfed in flame. Thick smoke billowed out, making it impossible to see across the stage.

Fortune began to cough. Her eyes were smarting. She let go of Mrs. Watson to rub them, only to find that made things worse. In the distance she could hear people screaming.

She reached for Mrs. Watson again, but the woman was gone. Fortune stumbled forward, her arms stretched before her. The smoke was so dense she couldn't see. Where were the others?

A momentary break in the smoke showed her that ahead and to her left Mr. Patchett was leading Walter toward the door.

Where are Aaron and Edmund? And what's happened to Mrs. Watson?

Suddenly a sound caught at Fortune's throat. She recognized Nancy Conaway's voice. The child was trapped somewhere in the loft, crying for help.

Lifting her skirt in front of her face, Fortune made her way in the direction of the child's cries. The heat was intense, searing her skin, her lungs. A spark caught at the edge of her dress. With a strength born of terror she tore off the outer skirt and threw it away from her, grateful for the trousers she wore beneath it.

Nancy shouted for help again.

"Where are you?" cried Fortune, coughing on the smoke that billowed around her.

"Here!" screamed the child. "Here!"

Suddenly Fortune could see her. Racing forward, she swept the child into her arms. Nancy flung herself around Fortune's neck and clung to her desperately.

Fortune turned and began to stumble toward the front of the loft. But the smoke was thicker now. She was choking and coughing, and her eyes were burning so fiercely she could hardly see. Yet she continued to move forward until a spurt of flame shot up beside her. She stopped. It was useless. She couldn't go on.

A beam fell from the roof, crashing nearby.

Nancy let out a cry of terror and squeezed Fortune's neck even more tightly. The terror of the helpless thing in her arms seemed to give Fortune new strength. Ducking her head, she forced herself to take another ten steps.

But the smoke was too much for her. She felt herself begin to sway.

Then someone reached out to take the child from her arms. Relieved of her burden, Fortune sank to the floor, the flames swirling around her.

CHAPTER FOUR

Strong arms folded about Fortune. Someone lifted her from the floor.

Aaron! she thought deliriously. *He knew I was in trouble and came back to get me.*

The flames were still roaring. The smoke was thick and choking. But she was safe. Resting her head against his chest, she drifted in and out of consciousness, content to let him take care of her now.

A dull explosion thundered somewhere behind them. Ahead, another beam crashed to the floor. She let out a scream that was stifled because her mouth was pressed against his chest. She heard him curse and was racked by a sudden fear that they were both going to die.

"Look out!" cried a voice from somewhere far away. She felt the muscles in his arms tighten, a lurch as he jumped, a moment of terrible heat, and then a sudden draft of cooler air.

They were out!

He swayed for a moment, as if about to faint, then stood solid again. Fortune opened her eyes. The glare from the blazing building seemed to blind her. It didn't matter. She drew her arms tighter about his neck and pulled herself closer to him. "Thank you," she whispered.

Then she kissed him, savoring the soft warmth of his lips against hers.

"Thank *you*, Miss Plunkett," he said when she drew away.

"You!" she cried in horror. She couldn't believe it. She had been rescued by Jamie Halleck. "Put me down, you . . . you *impostor!*"

A burst of laughter erupted around them. "Looks like you rescued a wildcat, Jamie," said one of the men.

"Draw in your claws, girl," said a voice close beside her. "The boy saved your life."

Smiling, Jamie set her down, then turned and walked away.

"Get back!" cried a voice. "Get back, it's about to go!"

Fortune rushed back with the throng of men as the general store began to collapse in on itself. The wooden frame shook, held steady for another moment, almost as if it had been frozen, then tumbled in like a house of cards before a sneeze.

A cascade of sparks swept into the sky, swirling up as if they were heading for the stars, going to become stars.

Fortune had no time to watch the spectacle. She had to find the others. Grabbing the sleeve of a nearby man, she cried, "Did everyone get out?"

He ignored her, his eyes locked on the blazing building.

Fortune followed his gaze. To her horror she saw that the buildings on either side of it were on fire now, too. She shook his arm. *"Did everyone get out all right?"*

About the time that she realized she was screaming, she recognized that the man she was talking to was Arthur MacKenzie, owner of the building that had just fallen. The loss had left him in a stupor.

She turned away, thinking she would have to ask someone else. With her first step she realized that she was still trembling. And the horrible truth was beginning to sink in on her: If any of the troupe hadn't gotten out, it was too late. They were dead.

She forced the thought from her mind. They couldn't lose anyone else. Not now. But in her near delirium the faces of her friends began to swirl before her, merging with the flames, screaming. She was about to scream herself when someone grabbed her by the arm. "Get in line!" yelled the stranger. "Do your part!"

With a start Fortune realized that the townspeople had formed a bucket brigade and were trying to keep the fire from spreading any farther. The general store was lost. But while the saloon to the right of it had caught fire, it could still be saved. The little church to the left was starting to go, too. It also needed instant attention.

Two lines of people stretched from the small river at the edge of town to the buildings. Fortune took her place in a spot where a gap was slowing things down. A bucket was thrust into her hands. She passed it to the next person in line. Almost before she could turn back, another bucket was being pressed on her. She passed that on, too, and the next, and the next.

Soon the routine became a mechanical blur. With her body working automatically, her thoughts wandered elsewhere. She tried to think about the others. But her mind kept betraying her, and she found herself remembering the feel of Jamie Halleck's arms around her body, the warmth and the softness of his lips when she had foolishly kissed him. *Why couldn't it have been Aaron?* she thought bitterly.

Her arms began to ache, but there was no time to rest. The buckets had to keep moving.

Fortune would have been amazed if she could have seen herself. When the evening began she was beautiful. "Radiant," as her father had often said. Now her costume was in tatters, the bottom half of it ripped off to reveal the trousers she wore beneath it for one of her Act Three scene changes. Her blond hair hung limply against a face smeared dark with smoke and dirt, and her arms and legs were nearly black.

And *still* the buckets kept coming. Her hands were starting to blister now, though she didn't realize it. The blisters formed, broke, formed again; the sharp pain there would not register until tomorrow.

Is this how the journey ends? she asked herself. *With a fire started by some drunken fool in a loft over a general store?* Tears began to course down her cheeks, cutting through the soot and ash. Her father had had such great plans for Plunkett's Players, so much he wanted them to do. He had left the task in her hands, and now—

"Don't be stupid," she said aloud, talking to herself but startling the woman who was passing her a bucket. "You haven't even looked for the others yet." She passed the bucket on. Her arms ached so that she wanted to die.

She took the next bucket, and the next, and the next. Then she reached out and to her surprise found nothing to grab. She turned. The fire was out.

She felt herself sway. *Stop it!* she thought sternly. She had no time for weakness now; she had to find the others. She took a deep breath, then another. Before she had to decide what to do next, Mr. Patchett appeared at her side.

"Fortune! Thank God you're all right!" he cried.

Then he put his arm around her and led her to a clearing.

To her relief, the others had already gathered there.

Weary to the bone, but exhilarated that they had all survived, Plunkett's Players stumbled back to Myra Halleck's boardinghouse, talking about what they had done, how they had survived.

Fortune was dragged from her exhausted sleep by a pounding on her door. She pulled the covers over her head. The pounding didn't stop.

"Go away!" she shouted.

Mrs. Watson let out a snort and flopped over, draping her arm across Fortune's chest. Fortune pushed it off.

And still the pounding continued. With a sigh she heaved aside the covers and got to her feet, flinching at the cold floor.

I can't believe someone is still up after everything

that's gone on tonight, she thought wearily.

Another burst of pounding thundered through the room. In exasperation she threw the door open to see who was there and was horrified to find Jamie Halleck, his eyes bright, his face still smeared with smoke. She put her hand to her cheek and realized that she was probably equally sooty, since she had been too tired to wash after they made their way back to the house.

"Go away," she said.

She tried to close the door, but he had thrust his foot inside and it jammed against his boot. "You have to pack at once," he said quietly. "I have your wagon hitched and ready to go."

She yanked the door open. "What are you talking about?"

Jamie looked embarrassed. "Some of the men are blaming you for the fire."

"That's ridiculous! Those two drunks caused all the trouble!"

"I didn't say it made sense," replied Jamie patiently. "I just told you what's happening. If you're smart you'll get dressed and get out of town before they do something crazy."

The blood drained from Fortune's face. She had seen small-town mobs before. She remembered one group of men, enraged over something much smaller than this, erupting into a rampage that had left two men dead. The look on Jamie's face told her this mob might prove equally dangerous.

"I've woken the others," he continued. "They're getting ready now."

"You should have woken me first! It's my troupe!"

"I'll have your wagon at the south edge of town in fifteen minutes," said Jamie curtly. "Be there!"

He turned and walked away.

Men! fumed Fortune. She crossed to the bed and shook Mrs. Watson. "Wake up," she said. "Wake up! We have to go."

Mrs. Watson snorted and rolled over.

Fortune shook the older woman again. "Wake up, Mrs. Watson. We have to get out of town."

As if Fortune's words had penetrated the fog of sleep, Mrs. Watson instantly sat bolt upright. "Oh, Minerva!" she cried. "It's just like the old days."

Throwing aside the covers, she sprang out of bed with a speed that astonished Fortune. Her red hair billowing around her like a cloud at sunset, she hummed cheerfully as she began throwing on her clothes. "Grab those dresses, duckie," she commanded. "Just throw them in there like that. Thank you!"

"Don't you want to know why we're leaving?" asked Fortune.

"It's because those two drunks started the fire, I would imagine."

"How did you know that?"

"It's part of an actor's life, chicken. You'll learn when you've been on the road a bit longer."

"Well, I don't like being blamed for something that wasn't our fault."

"You're not the first," said Mrs. Watson. "And you won't be the last. Best get packing or we won't make it."

Fortune sighed and threw her own clothes into her bag. Suddenly she sank down on the bed. "The costumes!" she moaned. "The properties. They were all burned. What are we going to do?"

"We'll *make* do," snapped Mrs. Watson. "Get moving!"

Struck by the note of urgency in the older woman's voice, Fortune leaped to her feet and finished packing. The properties and costumes would wait till another day.

They slipped into the hall. Edmund was there already, looking surly. Soon Aaron joined him. "Mr. Patchett and Walter have gone downstairs to make sure the coast is clear," he whispered. "Come on."

Moving in single file, the actors tiptoed along the hall to the stairwell at the south end. A board creaked once beneath Aaron's foot, startling Fortune so much that she almost dropped her bag.

"Shhh!" hissed Mrs. Watson, who was walking right behind her.

"I'm trying!" snapped Fortune.

Walter loomed at the base of the stairs, an anxious look deepening the lines of his face. "Mr. Patchett has gone on ahead," he whispered, scratching nervously at his beard. "When he sees us come out of the house, he'll move on a way to make sure it's safe." He looked the group over anxiously. "Ready?"

They all nodded.

Walter opened the door carefully, striving not to make any noise. Fortune looked behind her. At least they had paid in advance, she thought with grim satisfaction. Actors might be notorious for sneaking out of boardinghouses without paying, but Plunkett's Players had never done it, and she didn't want to start now.

That thought led her mind to another matter.

"The money! Walter, did—"

"Shhhh!" hissed Mrs. Watson. Fortune fumed. Was the money safe, or had it been lost in the fire?

Without further sound they passed into the darkness. It was a cool night, quiet and calm. The stars were bright and clear, the spring constellations twinkling as if nothing horrible had happened here. In the distance peepers were singing their chorus. A light dew coated the ground. But the odor of smoke still filled the air. Fortune shuddered; the smell brought memories of the ordeal in the loft flooding over her.

A series of shouts in the distance reminded her that the night was not as calm as it seemed here in the darkness behind Halleck's boardinghouse.

She heard a rustling in the bushes ahead of them—Mr. Patchett moving on. After a moment he made an owl-like sound. The troupe moved forward. Before long they had reached his side. It frightened Fortune to see how worried he was.

When he had counted to be sure they were all there, he moved on again. Soon the owl sound drifted through the night. They followed his path once more.

Traveling in this fashion they came to a clearing at the edge of town. There, standing in a pool of moonlight, was Jamie Halleck. He held the reins of the lead pair of the troupe's team, which he had already harnessed to their wagon. The silvery light caught in his chestnut hair, making it appear like some strangely cool fire. A flicker of a smile played over his lips.

"Good work, lad," said Mr. Patchett, striding to his side. He took the reins from Jamie.

"I don't know how we can ever repay you," said Walter, stepping up beside him. "You have done us a great favor."

"Take me with you," said Jamie simply.

"You must be out of your mind!" cried Edmund.

"I was not speaking to you," said Jamie. "I was addressing Miss Plunkett." He turned to Fortune. "I would like to be allowed to accompany your troupe on its trip to San Francisco. I will work hard and help you in whatever way I can."

The simple request was obviously difficult for him to make, and she realized with sudden certainty that he had never asked anyone for a favor before.

Jamie was gazing at her intently. She saw nothing childlike or moonstruck about him. But his eyes, large and warm, were pleading with her.

She thought about the harpy he lived with. In the short time they had been there, Fortune had seen and heard enough to know that Mrs. Halleck made her son's life a living torment. It was so strangely different from the way her parents had treated her that she had hardly been able to understand it. She knew that Jamie would never turn on his mother, never lash out at her. But he would leave the woman. Fortune's mind took the next step forward and realized that not only would he leave her, but that he had to do so. And they were his best hope for making that break.

Jamie smiled, and her heart ached as she realized what a gallant gesture it was.

What do I do? He's acting like it doesn't really matter. But I can see how much it does. She swallowed and faced the hard fact. *He wouldn't dream of mentioning that I owe him my life. But I do.*

"Look, it was nice of you to help us," said Aaron curtly. "But you'd better . . ."

"You'd better be ready if you're planning on coming with us," said Fortune, using the tone of voice that said *I* am the leader of this troupe.

For a moment she was dazzled by the smile that broke across Jamie's face, the joy she read in his eyes. Then he nodded slightly, and said, "Much obliged, miss," as if it was nothing at all.

He hurried to the side of the clearing and came back leading a horse. It was already saddled, and there was a rifle strapped to its side. He had a carpetbag in his hand and a bundle of books under his arm.

"What are those?" asked Mrs. Watson, always curious at the sight of printed matter.

Jamie smiled. "My Shakespeare!"

"Oh, dear God," sighed Edmund, putting his hands together, as if in prayer. "Be merciful to your humble servants and spare us from would-be actors!"

CHAPTER FIVE

When they were far enough from the town, Jamie filled them in on the events that had followed the fire. He was riding next to the wagon, and his voice came out of the cold darkness. He spoke clearly to be heard above the creaking of the wagon.

"It started with the keg of whiskey someone broke out to thank the folks who helped put out the fire," he said. "I suppose the men did deserve a drink. But it didn't take long before there was a fair number of them as drunk as those two who started the trouble to begin with."

"That doesn't surprise me," said Fortune bitterly.

Jamie paused long enough to make her wonder what he was thinking, then went on with his story.

"Poor Mr. MacKenzie was the worst of the lot. He was awful bitter. I can understand: This morning he owned a store, and now all he has is a pile of ashes. But he seemed to take it pretty personal. Anyway, he finally got up and made a speech about what you folks had done to him that got the others as riled up as he was.

"I could tell they were getting a big mad on. I tried to talk them out of it; pointed out that Fortune had saved little Nancy Conaway's life, and that all of you had worked on the bucket brigades. They weren't having any of that. Even so, I thought it might blow over—until some of them went out looking for tar and feathers. That's when I decided I'd better come and roust you out."

Fortune shuddered at the nearness of their escape.

She was glad to be free of the town, which she had disliked from the moment she arrived there. And she was relieved that Walter had been able to save the night's take. But she was deeply troubled that she had not found out why her father had wanted them to go to Busted Heights to begin with. His unfinished business would have to remain unfinished, and that bothered her.

They traveled until morning, when they found a place to get out of sight of the road in a small stand of trees next to a stream. They washed up in the cold water, glad to rid themselves of the stink of the smoke, which still clung to their skin and hair.

The men took shifts standing guard a few miles up the road, in case the angry townspeople decided to pursue them. When darkness fell they began to travel again. They drove through Smith's Corners, the next town along the road, without stopping.

Two days of hard travel later, they reached Bevins.

It was the last town they planned to stop in before they reached Independence, where they were to join Abner Simpson's wagon train to make the journey across the plains and over the Rocky Mountains to California.

Bevins was a pleasant surprise after the string of increasingly dreary settlements that had led them to Busted Heights. Not only was it larger and more prosperous looking than the last several places they had been; but somehow it seemed to have an air of friendliness about it.

Moreover, Fortune no longer felt like a fugitive.

"That could be just because we're far enough from Busted Heights to stop worrying about revenge," pointed out Mrs. Watson when Fortune expressed this feeling.

Whatever the reason, she felt more comfortable as she looked the town over.

We've nearly reached the end of the beginning, she

thought, looking around the town. *One more town and the real journey begins. I wish you were still with us, Papa.*

They gathered the next afternoon in a space not unlike the site of their catastrophic performance in Busted Heights. The fact that they had had no problem finding a place suitable to put on a show confirmed that word of their last performance had not yet traveled this far west.

As Fortune listened with growing anxiety to the argument developing between Mr. Patchett and Mrs. Watson, she began to think that finding a place to work had been the easy part.

"You can't possibly expect me to do that, Henry!" cried Mrs. Watson. "It is an insult to my talent!"

Mr. Patchett sighed. "My dear Mrs. Watson, all I am suggesting is that you play the scene exactly the way you did the last ninety-six times we performed this show!"

"It's *not* the same, and I won't do it! The whole production is wrong anyway. We have no sense of style, no sense of elegance. Now, here's what I think—"

"Woman, I do not *care* what you think! Will you please take your position before I lose my temper completely?"

Fortune sighed. At least things were back to some semblance of normality. With Jamie's arrival the troupe had decided to attempt a different play, since they were all thoroughly tired of *The Widow's Daughter.* Though his work would be limited to walk-ons and lines like, "Yes, Your Majesty," his very presence freed up one of the other actors to take on some larger parts.

She glanced over to where Jamie stood at the edge of the makeshift stage, waiting to make his entrance. Aaron gave him his cue. Fortune winced as she watched Jamie bolt awkwardly up the steps, stumble, and blurt out his line so fast that it seemed like one long word.

"No, no, no," said Mrs. Watson. "Here, try it like this."

"Madam," said Mr. Patchett, "are you directing this play or am I?" Though he spoke softly, there was murder in his voice.

"Oh, what difference does it make, Henry?" she asked airily. "We're just trying to get it to come out right, aren't we, ducky?" Her second comment, addressed to Jamie, was accompanied by a squeeze of his cheek.

"I guess so," he said, looking very uncomfortable.

Fortune could sympathize. She had been caught in the Patchett-Watson crossfire herself, and she knew it was no fun. Worse, it had been going on all afternoon. She could see Mr. Patchett's usually good temper wearing thin.

"Looks like your boyfriend is going to make a mess of things," said Edmund, sidling up beside her.

"He's not my boyfriend!" Fortune snapped. "And I think he's doing perfectly well, all things considered."

Edmund gave her an evil grin and walked toward the stage.

Wondering what he was up to, Fortune found herself wishing again that they had never let him join the group. Suddenly she realized her entrance was coming up. She lifted her skirts to head for the stage. Halfway there she stopped, surprised by an unfamiliar line. After a moment she realized that Edmund was delivering a fake cue. Aaron picked up on it, and sent the dialogue spinning off into nowhere.

Jamie looked from one to the other, his eyes wide with panic.

Mr. Patchett, who had turned aside to make a note of something, looked up. A puzzled frown wrinkled his face. "Jamie? . . ."

"Uh . . . uh . . ."

He looked frantically out at Fortune.

Aaron erupted in gleeful laughter.

"It's not funny!" said Jamie sharply.

"I should say not!" snapped Mrs. Watson. "Henry, you should see to—oh, never mind, I'll do it. Now, look here, Edmund. If you and Aaron think—"

"Mrs. Watson," said Mr. Patchett, "would you please—"

"Be quiet, Henry. This is important!"

Fortune caught her breath.

Mr. Patchett's face turned an odd shade of red. Without a word he stalked onto the stage. Silence filled the room, the kind of quiet that prevails before a tornado. Mrs. Watson's air of grand control was replaced by a nervous expression.

Mr. Patchett stood before her without speaking for a moment.

He's going to hit her! thought Fortune, horrified by the thought, yet fascinated at the idea. To her disgust she found herself, as she often did, wondering how she could use this moment onstage. She shook the idea away.

However, Mr. Patchett had no intention of hitting anyone. Instead he bent and began to undo his shoelaces.

"Madam," he said gravely, "as it is obvious you will never be happy until you have filled my shoes, I will give them to you."

As he spoke he slipped off his brogues and kicked them toward Mrs. Watson's feet. The actress said nothing, but her lower lip began to tremble. Walter jumped to his feet. Mr. Patchett waved him aside and continued his speech.

"Furthermore, it is clear that you will never rest until you are the one who wears the pants in this organization. Therefore, let me give you these, also."

Unbuckling his trousers, he dropped them to the floor. After stepping deftly out, he picked them up and tossed them in her direction. "I hope they fit," he said sweetly. He turned to the others. "As there is obviously no further need for me today, I shall be in my room. Please call me when it is time for dinner."

His shirttail flapping around his skinny bare legs, he turned and stalked out of the hall with all the dignity of one of the crowned heads of Europe.

The members of the troupe looked at one another. After a moment of stunned silence Mrs. Watson—who had caught Mr. Patchett's pants—dropped them as if they had suddenly threatened to bite her.

Suddenly Fortune realized just how funny the expression on Mrs. Watson's face was. She began to laugh, a rollicking release of mirth that was soon joined by the others—all save Mrs. Watson. She gazed at them in growing horror, her cheeks turning crimson. "Philistines!" she cried. Then she turned and fled the room.

After a moment Jamie ran after her.

Suddenly Fortune realized what kind of problem she had on her hands. The rehearsal was ruined. And if she couldn't pull the group back together, the performance would be, too. Turning to Aaron, she snapped, "Now look what you've done!"

"Me?" he said, the essence of wounded innocence. "What did I do?"

"Oh, forget it!" she snapped.

The last thing she saw before she left the room was the puzzled expression on his face.

Mrs. Watson sat beneath an oak tree, sobbing convulsively. Jamie knelt beside her, his hand on her shoulder, talking quietly.

Stepping softly, Fortune moved closer.

"It was kind of you to stick up for me," said Jamie to Mrs. Watson.

"They . . . they were laughing at you."

"I know," said Jamie. "I'm used to it."

"How can you stand it?" wailed Mrs. Watson. "That's why I ran out. *They were laughing at me, too! AT ME!*" Throwing her arms around Jamie's neck, she buried her face in his shoulder.

He disentangled himself, then pulled a handkerchief from his pocket—a large red bandanna, utterly different from the tiny lace ones Mrs. Watson was so fond of. He began to dab at her eyes.

Look at how gentle he is, thought Fortune.

A terrible thought struck her. She remembered just the other night thinking that Mrs. Watson was very attractive for her age. Could it be that he was interested in her?

Fortune stamped her foot, impatient with her own foolishness. Mrs. Watson was old enough to be his mother for heaven's sake. Anyway, it made no difference to her. Jamie could like Mrs. Watson, or that girl who was with him the night of the fire, or his horse, for all she cared.

She bit her lip. Even so, she wished Aaron would show her some of the kind of tenderness that Jamie was now demonstrating. No one ever held her when she wanted to cry. Not that she would ever let anyone see her in that condition. She was leader of the troupe, and if she was going to get them to California she had to be strong, to lock away—

"Fortune!"

She gasped. Mrs. Watson had spotted her. Embarrassed at what might appear to be eavesdropping, Fortune stammered, "I . . . I just came out to see if you were all right. I feel badly that—that your feelings were hurt."

"It's perfectly all right," said Mrs. Watson,

mustering her dignity. "I was simply taken aback by the rudeness of some people. Fortunately, not everyone is like that." She looked fondly at Jamie.

"I know what it's like," said Jamie quietly. "That's all."

She patted his cheek. "Well, I want to give you some private coaching. We'll show those yahoos who can act and who can't. By the time I'm through with you, Aaron and Edmund will look like such amateurs they'll be ashamed to be on the same stage with you."

Fortune stifled a groan. As if she didn't have troubles enough already!

Deciding she needed some advice, she headed for the only place she could be sure of finding a sympathetic ear.

CHAPTER SIX

Romeo and Juliet were quietly munching their oats when Fortune slipped into the dimly lit stable. Motes of dust danced in the shafts of light that came through the cracks in the walls. The air was heavy with barn smells—horse sweat, manure, musty hay—all blending into an unlikely perfume that she found oddly pleasant.

Guess I'm just a country girl at heart, Fortune thought.

She snorted at her own foolishness. She wasn't a country girl, and she knew it.

But what was she? John and Laura Plunkett's orphan daughter. A child of the stage. Heir to an acting tradition that stretched back, her father claimed, over a hundred years. And now, by accident and tragedy, the leader of a band of traveling players following a possibly hopeless dream of building their own theater in the golden land of California.

What else was she?

Lonely.

The word popped into her head unbidden, surprising her. How could she be lonely, when she had the troupe?

But she was. Well, that was why she had come here—to talk to Romeo and Juliet, her sole confidantes. Romeo was the better listener, but Juliet gave better advice . . . at least in the dialogues that Fortune constructed for them.

She climbed onto the side of the stall, well aware of how horrified Mrs. Watson would be if she could see her sitting here in such an "unladylike" fashion.

Romeo lifted his head and poked his muzzle against her, looking for a treat.

"Sorry, friend, nothing today but a bit of affection." She rubbed his nose, which was velvety soft except for an occasional bristle.

Juliet, instantly jealous, poked her head against Fortune, also.

"Well, what do you think?" she asked, addressing both horses.

Juliet whickered softly.

"Oh, I'm sorry," said Fortune. "I haven't told you the latest developments, have I?"

Romeo shook his head.

"Your timing is improving," said Fortune. She grimaced. "Now there's a perfect example of one part of the problem. I think about *everything* from a theatrical viewpoint. I don't want to do that. I'd rather be normal sometimes!"

Juliet shook her head and blew air through her lips.

"What do you mean, it's hopeless?" asked Fortune, her voice filled with mock indignation. "I can be normal if I try!"

She looked at the horse for a moment, then sighed. "I guess the idea is pretty far-fetched, isn't it?"

Romeo neighed loudly.

"Well, you don't have to be that way about it," said Fortune. "I know it's in my blood. I'm not denying my heritage. But it's not *all* that I want out of life." She sighed again. "The others all *chose* to be in the theater. Heck, Walter couldn't live without it. But I never made that choice. No one asked me. It was just my luck that I was born into an acting family. Not that I don't like it. I just wish it wasn't the only thing I knew."

She scratched Romeo behind his ears. "Anyway, that's not what's bothering me right now." She glanced at the stable door, then relaxed. She had managed to train the others to leave her alone when she went off to be with the horses.

"It's that Jamie Halleck," she said. "Even though he's just a big pain in the neck, I can't get him out of my mind. I know Aaron is the man for me. But when I saw Jamie with Mrs. Watson out there—and just between us, you should have seen how gooey she was acting!—I felt something twist inside me. I know he's only a bumpkin, but there's something about him . . . something—"

"Dreadfully charming?" asked a husky voice behind her.

Fortune spun around so fast she nearly fell off the edge of the stall. Romeo, startled, reared back, pawing the air with his hooves.

"Whoa!" cried Jamie. "Easy, boy."

At the same time his hands shot out to steady Fortune. With one hand behind her back and the other on her arm, he held her until she was secure again.

"You'd better watch it!" he said, leaving his hand against her back just an instant longer than was necessary. "This would be a terrible place to fall while you're wearing such a pretty dress."

Fortune smiled in spite of herself. Then she remembered his interruption. "What are *you* doing here?" she demanded. She followed the question immediately with another, more urgent one: "And how long have you been listening?"

She tried to fight down the blush she felt creeping up her cheeks as she recalled the things she had said. The blush grew deeper when she realized that Jamie must have known she was talking to the horses.

Jamie gave her a crooked smile, and Fortune could see what her mother had often called "the look of the devil" in his eyes. Laura Plunkett had used the phrase to describe sophisticated young men of great charm and humor when they were feeling impish. Again, Fortune found herself confused. That look, which she found wildly attractive, was something she had never expected to find in a country boy.

"I came in just a second ago," said Jamie, answering her question. "About the time you were saying 'He's only a bumpkin.'" He flashed her a rakish grin. "Of course, I knew at once you must be talking about me. Then I heard you say 'There's something about him . . . something . . .' I wasn't sure what was coming next, so I figured I'd better finish the sentence for you—before you could come up with something really dreadful!"

Fortune looked at him suspiciously.

"Cross my heart!" said Jamie, holding up his hand as if taking an oath. "That's all I heard!"

She didn't know whether to smile back or dump a handful of oats on his head.

"May I?" he asked while she was trying to make up her mind. He was gesturing toward the spot beside her on the stall wall. Without waiting for her answer, he climbed up and sat beside her. "You're lucky," he said, cutting off her objection. "Horses are sensible creatures to converse with . . ."

Fortune could feel herself flare. "Why, you—"

"Wait! I'm not finished. As I said, you're lucky. Until I got Dolly, whenever *I* wanted someone to talk to, I had to go out in the backyard and bare my soul to the chickens!"

He glanced at her out of the corner of his eye. Fortune tried, unsuccessfully, to hide her smile.

"Do you know what it's like to share your innermost feelings with a chicken?" he continued, a note of mock-tragedy in his voice. "Do you know what kind of advice you get? *Ba-gawk ba-gawk ba-gawk!*"

Fortune began to smirk. Jamie's raucous imitation of a chicken was breaking down the tension she had felt building within her. Suddenly she began to laugh.

Her reaction spurred him on. Springing down from the wall, he began to enact a conversation between himself and one of his mother's hens.

"So, Matilda, what do you think I should do about my life? It's not easy living with Madame Medusa, you know."

Squatting down, he tucked his hands into his armpits and looked up at where he had been standing. *"Ba-gawk,"* he said, blinking and flapping his imaginary wings. *"Ba-gawk-gawk-gawk."*

He jumped to his feet. "Oh, no, Matilda. I *can't* step on mother's eggs. Besides, she doesn't lay any!"

He squatted down and began to squawk again, carrying on a dialogue so ridiculous and so hilarious that soon Fortune was laughing so hard she could scarcely breathe.

"Stop!" she gasped. "Stop!"

She pressed her hands to her stomach and as a result almost fell off the wall again. Jamie leaped up and put out a hand to steady her.

This time she didn't flinch away.

"So you can see why I consider you lucky," he concluded, as if he had never been imitating a chicken. "At least a horse is a sensible animal."

He let go of her, then jumped up to sit beside her on the wall again.

"All right," said Fortune when she had caught her breath. "I'll grant you that a horse is better than a hen for sharing your innermost feelings." She paused and looked at him intently. "But people can be even better."

"When you can trust them."

"Are most people that untrustworthy?"

"There are different kinds of trust. Even if you can trust a person not to shout a secret to the world, it doesn't mean you can trust him to understand what you're talking about."

The note of aching loneliness in his voice made Fortune want to reach out and comfort him. She beat down the thought. If he was going to be traveling with them, it was a good idea to get to know him. That didn't mean acting like his mother!

Yet at the same time another part of her knew exactly how he felt. It was so damn lonely when there was no one to listen to your dreams, no one to share your secrets. She turned to him. "I . . ."

"Yes?"

The words froze in her throat as she realized that her fears were the same as his. What made her think she could trust him more than anyone else? Because he was lonely, too? Because he looked like a lost puppy when he had that expression in his eyes? Those things didn't make someone safe.

"Never mind," she said weakly.

Jamie turned away. "You think I'm pretty foolish, don't you?"

"No! Not at all!"

He turned back. "You can't trust someone unless you know they're willing to tell you the truth. That wasn't it."

Fortune's temper flared—partly because he had accused her of lying, partly because he was right. She *was* lying, and she didn't like being caught.

"All right. I was trying to spare your feelings. But the truth is, you do seem pretty foolish to me—and I imagine to the rest of them as well." Her voice took on a sarcastic tone as she added, "With the possible exception of Mrs. Watson."

An odd expression crossed his face. Unable to interpret its meaning, Fortune rolled on. "If you want the truth, there it is. What kind of person would run off to join a troupe of actors—especially when that person has no acting experience himself? You *have* to be crazy!"

The expression on Jamie's face was almost amused now. "That's just the point. I *am* crazy. Aren't you?"

"No! I didn't go looking for this gypsy life. My parents were actors, and when they died I inherited the troupe. This is my living. It's what I do."

He looked at her sadly. "I'm sorry about your parents. I know something about what that's like."

Neither of them spoke for a moment. Finally Jamie cleared his throat and said, "How did it happen?"

She shook her head. "I don't want to talk about it."

"All right. What do you want to talk about?"

Fortune was silent for a moment. She didn't want to talk at all. She just wanted to sit and be quiet. It was nice to be with someone else who was lonely, someone else who knew what it was to lose a parent. She sighed. Probably he would think she was stupid if she didn't say something.

"Let's talk about you. How did you end up so in love with 'the theater' that you were willing to run away from home for it?"

He made a face. "Wasn't much of a home to run away from. Besides, I *should* be out on my own by now. A lot of people our age are already married and settled down."

"That doesn't answer my question. And how old are you?"

"Which question do you want me to answer?"

"Both."

"I'm eighteen. And you're right, I skirted your other question. It was my father. He loved the theater. I think in his secret heart he wanted to be an actor. Or maybe a playwright. Whatever it was he truly wanted to do, it wasn't to be found in Busted Heights."

"Then why was he there?"

"My mother," said Jamie bitterly. "My step-mother, to be totally accurate, though she was all the mother I ever knew. My real mother was gone long before I can remember. Anyway, I don't know a lot about what brought them out here, just bits and pieces of information my father dropped when we were talking. I wish I had asked him more, before he . . ." He stopped for a moment, to collect his emotions. "Funny thing. You always think you'll have all the time in the world to ask those questions. Anyway, they lived back East when they were young. So did I, for that matter. I was born in Philadelphia."

"That's where I was born!"

Jamie smiled. "Obviously they know how to have children of the finest kind in that city. But whatever else Pa was doing besides having me, he wasn't successful at it. So he and Ma headed west to try to make a go of things, settled in Busted Heights, and then just kind of withered and died."

"But I thought your mother—your step-mother—was still alive. Wasn't that her boarding-house?"

"You can call that living if you want. I don't. She's a bitter, shrill old woman. Except she's not really old; she just acts and thinks that way." He paused, and when he continued his voice was cold. "I know I shouldn't talk that way about the woman who raised me. But I can't help it. She killed my father."

Fortune sucked in her breath.

"Oh, not literally," he said quickly. "But I believe Pa would still be alive if it weren't for her forcing him to give up everything he loved." He stopped to get control of his emotions. When he began again, he was calmer, as if he had hidden something away. "You asked about the theater. My father's most precious possessions were his books of Shakespeare. They were the only things he owned that he really cared about. He used to read to me from them, starting when I was little. But once Ma started getting religion, we couldn't let her hear, on account of she thought any kind of playacting was the devil's work. So we had to sneak off whenever we wanted to read together. We had a couple of secret places we liked to go."

Fortune began to understand why Jamie loved his books so much. The expression on his face when he talked about them cut right to her heart. He looked just as her father used to when *he* got talking about the theater.

"Of course," continued Jamie, "Ma would be furious whenever she caught Pa reading to me. That only happened in the winter, when we had to do it in the barn instead of outside. But despite all the screaming and shouting, neither of us was willing to give it up. We used to read the plays over and over, acting them out together. I know a lot of them by heart."

"You don't, either!"

"Try me."

Rummaging through her mind, Fortune

dragged up a line from *Romeo and Juliet* that she had always enjoyed for its wild romanticism. "All right, try this. It's Romeo speaking. 'I am no pilot; yet wert thou as far as that vast shore . . .'"

Jamie paused for a moment. Then he nodded, as if he had caught the thread. Jumping to the floor, he stared up at her, stared directly into her eyes. For one strange moment, sitting there on that rough stable wall, Fortune had the sense of *being* Juliet on her balcony—with the dearest man in all the world standing below her.

"'I am no pilot,'" said Jamie, his voice deep and resonant, his brown eyes boring into hers. "'Yet wert thou as far as that vast shore, wash'd with the farthest sea, I would adventure for such merchandise.'"

Fortune turned her eyes away, astonished that he knew the line—and even more astonished by the truth in his voice when he delivered it.

Confused, and a little frightened, she cut short the conversation. "That's very good. I'd like to hear you do more someday. But I have to go now. I . . . I promised Mr. Patchett I would help him try to figure out how to replace some of the properties we lost in the fire."

Jamie nodded, and Fortune hurried from the stable, which had suddenly begun to feel as dangerous as a burning theater.

CHAPTER SEVEN

Fortune was heading toward their lodgings when Aaron fell into step beside her. Anger darkened his eyes. "What were you doing in there?"

"In where?"

"In the stable, with—with *him.*"

Fortune could hardly believe her ears. *What do you care?* was the first thought that flashed through her mind. Biting back the bitter retort she said, "We were talking. Why?"

"He's . . . not good for you. He'll fill your head with foolish notions."

Fortune laughed out loud. "What in heaven's name has gotten into you?"

"Nothing!" He ran his fingers through his curly black hair, as if the action would help him answer her question. "I just don't want to see you make a fool out of yourself."

It was Fortune's turn to flare. "I am perfectly capable of taking care of myself, Mr. Masters. Kindly tend to your own business!"

She turned on her heel and stalked away from him. But she was not nearly as angry as she had pretended to be. How could she be, when he was finally showing some sign of interest in her? Was he actually jealous of Jamie?

Too bad! She wasn't about to rearrange her life to suit Aaron Masters. If being friends with Jamie would make Aaron pay a little more attention to her . . . well, her father had always said friends were a person's most precious possession.

"Did you youngsters have a nice chat, chickie?"

Fortune blinked. She had been so intent on her own thoughts she hadn't noticed Mrs. Watson walking up beside her. The question had been almost purred. But there was an edge of steel in the voice that made Fortune wary. She had a momentary vision of the life of the entire troupe being disrupted by the presence of the handsome young stranger.

She shook her head. She had to stop thinking like this. Mrs. Watson *couldn't* be interested in Jamie!

"Yes, we did have a nice chat," she said, as if nothing at all had crossed her mind. "We have a lot in common."

Mrs. Watson's face was expressionless.

That's the problem with living with actors, thought Fortune. *They spend their whole life pretending. So you never know what they're thinking unless they want you to.*

"I wonder if Mr. Patchett is still angry," she said aloud, mainly to change the subject.

Mrs. Watson rolled her eyes. "Of course not. I went and apologized to him."

"You what?" cried Fortune, stopping in midstride.

"I told the old fool I was sorry when I took back his shoes and pants. It was Jamie's suggestion. I think it was a good idea."

Fortune shook her head. Based on past performance, she would have expected the sun to rise in the west before Mrs. Watson apologized to Mr. Patchett for interfering with a rehearsal. Yet she had stated the fact as calmly as if saying she had decided to have an extra egg for breakfast.

Before she could think of how to respond, Walter came lumbering across the street to join them. Tipping his derby, he said, "We'll be late for supper if we're not careful."

He held out his arm. When Mrs. Watson slipped her hand into the crook of his elbow, he seemed to relax visibly. Even so, he caught Fortune's eye and without words asked her, *Have I got anything to worry about?*

"I can't stand it!" cried Fortune.

Walter and Mrs. Watson blinked in astonishment.

"Supper," said Fortune hastily. "This town is certainly an improvement over Busted Heights, but the food is just awful. I can't stand another meal here."

"Well, *I'm* famished!" said Mrs. Watson. She and Walter took off at a near gallop, heading for the boardinghouse.

Fortune crossed to a nearby tree and leaned against the rough, sturdy trunk. Until Jamie had joined them, the tensions and relationships in the troupe had been set and predictable. Some things were good, some were bad, but she had been able, for the most part, to predict how people would react. Edmund's arrival hadn't changed that; he was an irritant, of course, but nothing that they couldn't live with. But somehow Jamie was like a stick thrust into a pond and stirred around. Things were swirling. And who could tell where they would land when they finally settled down again?

On Saturday morning Plunkett's Players rolled out of Bevins and headed for Independence. Their performance of *The Squire and the Lady* the night before had been acceptable, though hardly inspired. It was the funniest play in their repertory, and at least they had gotten most of the laughs they expected.

The most notable aspect of the evening had been Jamie's sheer pleasure in the event. Aaron and Edmund had made a number of cynical comments about his wide-eyed enthusiasm. But Fortune had enjoyed it, partly because it had reminded her of how much she sometimes loved performing herself.

As usual, Aaron and Fortune sat at the front of the wagon, Aaron guiding Romeo and Juliet with his firm, steady hand. Jamie was riding his roan mare, Dolly, though occasionally he tied her to the back of the wagon and sat inside so that he could talk with the rest of the troupe.

Equally often, one or more of them would climb out of the wagon to stretch their legs by walking part of the way. Only Mrs. Watson rode the entire distance.

"I don't know how she does it," said Mr. Patchett to Fortune when they stopped to take a break. "If I sat like that for an entire day, my legs wouldn't work at all by the time we stopped for dinner."

Given the length of his legs, this didn't surprise Fortune. What she was more interested in was the way that he and Mrs. Watson had managed to patch up their differences. It was as if nothing at all had happened.

She had talked to Walter about it the previous night, during the first intermission. "Can a simple apology be that effective?" she had asked in amazement.

"If it's sincere," he said, looking down at her with his best kindly old bear expression. Then he broke into an impish grin and added, "Of course, it helps if it's totally unexpected and out of character."

Fortune had laughed. But the question still intrigued her. She had never been good at apologies herself. It always seemed so painful to admit she was wrong.

And the more wrong she was, the harder it got.

Well, it was something to think about. In the meantime, there was the trek west to be faced. She realized she had been *avoiding* thinking about it, partly because she knew it was going to be long and difficult. Her father had clipped many of the letters earlier overlanders had sent to the newspapers describing their experiences. He had also read the troupe long sections of Mr. Parkman's wonderful book *The Oregon Trail*, and she remembered vividly the hardships that it had described. Fortune did take some comfort in knowing the journey wouldn't be as rough now as it had been for the very first ones to cross.

Papa, are you watching over us? she thought. *This is really your trip after all.*

She turned away from that line of thought, which sometimes led to a bitterness for her father that she did not want to feel. Besides, it was no longer true. She had made the journey her own, and she had every intention of getting the troupe to San Francisco.

She turned her thoughts to the spring morning that surrounded them. The sky was as clear as crystal, as blue as a cornflower. The air was sweet and pure, the land covered with a veil of light green that was as lovely as anything she had seen in a long, long time. Suddenly she felt at peace with herself, and eager about the journey to come. They were going to cross territory that had been a mystery until the last few years, hardly seen by anyone other than Indians. It was an adventure!

She asked Walter to hand up her guitar. As the wagon jounced and the axles creaked and the horses plodded along, she began to pluck out the chords of the overlander's popular "Oh, Susanna."

After a moment, she began to sing. The others joined her, and the unexpectedly pleasant sound of Jamie Halleck's tenor voice harmonizing with Aaron's pure baritone sent a little chill running down her spine.

*   *   *

Even though Jamie had told them what to expect, Fortune's first sight of Independence left her amazed. The town was in the midst of its annual spring explosion, and permanent structures were far outnumbered by wagons filled with pilgrims ready to attempt the westward adventure. According to Jamie, Independence was one of the three main jumping-off places for wagon trains, and ever since the discovery of gold in California, hopeful travelers had gathered here each April to wait for the prairie mud to dry before launching their daring journey.

It's like a city without buildings, thought Fortune. *All these people, with nothing to live in but wagons.*

For the first time it really sank in that a wagon was what they, too, would be living in—or out of— for the next four or five months as they made their way to San Francisco. Until now they had stayed in boardinghouses except for those few nights when they had not been able to reach a town. On those occasions the men had slept under the stars—or under the wagon if it was raining—while she and Mrs. Watson shared the wagon floor.

Fortune smiled at the memory. One of the floorboards had a hole in it, and more than once she had been able to peek through and watch Aaron sleeping. She liked to look at him that way.

The hard expression left his face then, and his tousled hair was . . .

She shook herself out of her daydream. Sleeping in the wagon was no longer to be a once-in-a-while situation. It was the way they were going to live!

Fortune fought down a surge of panic and tried to think about what she had read of San Francisco—how it was a booming town to rival or even outstrip the most exciting cities in the East, a place where entertainers could find fame and fortune virtually overnight if they somehow caught the public fancy, and where gold was changing hands as fast as buckets in a bucket brigade.

Others have done it. We can, too.

Her brave words to herself were deflated by another small voice inside her, a voice that said, *They were outdoorsmen; we're actors. We know nothing about surviving in the wild.*

She tried to quell that fear by reminding herself that that was why they were joining a wagon train. The others would help them get through. . . .

Aaron guided the horses through the bustle of the streets to a spot at the edge of town where there was room to stake them out.

Mr. Patchett looked around at the crowded camp and sighed happily. "People, Fortune. Lots of people. And believe me, before this trip is over, they'll be bored and wanting entertainment. I wish your father was here, sweetheart. He would have loved this."

No sooner had the words passed his lips than it was clear he regretted them. Fortune said nothing, simply turned and looked back toward the east.

A few hours after they had found a place to rest, a lean, leather-skinned man with a long mustache and a stubble of white beard came striding over to their wagon.

"Take it you're the Plunkett group," he said. It was an easy assumption, given the fact that their name was boldly painted on their wagon cover. Fortune was a little embarrassed by the way it stood out among the sea of white wagon tops.

"We are indeed Plunkett's Players," said Mr. Patchett cheerfully.

The lean newcomer nodded seriously. "I'm Abner Simpson, your wagon master." He gazed around at the group, then shook his head in amazement. "I'll tell you honestly—I have seen unlikelier crews than this make it across in one piece. But not many." With a mournful note in his voice he asked, "You sure you want to do this?"

"Oh, Minerva!" moaned Mrs. Watson from the back of the wagon.

"Now, look here, my good man," said Mr.

Patchett, his good humor evaporating. "You are being paid to guide this wagon train across the continent. We are part of the train, and as such we expect your help and encouragement."

"I'll give you as much help as I give anyone else," said Simpson. "But don't count on encouragement. My daddy taught me it was nothing but cruelty to encourage fools."

"Just a minute!" said Fortune. "I don't—"

"Quiet, woman," snapped Simpson. He turned to Aaron and said, "Keep your wife out of my way. I don't like mouthy females."

"Yes, sir!" said Aaron, trying to hide a smirk. Fortune turned bright red. She would have spoken up, save for a look from Mr. Patchett that virtually begged her to hold her tongue.

The wagon master turned his horse and rode away from them. "Try to stay out of trouble till we go!" he called over his shoulder. Then he jerked his horse to a stop. "Better yet," he said, looking back toward them, "turn back while you still can!"

"Well, I like that!" said Mrs. Watson angrily. "Who does he think he is anyway? The pompous rooster!"

"You have to ignore him," said Jamie, struggling not to laugh. "Believe me, Simpson has seen worse than us cross the prairie. He's not nearly as bad as he sounds, or as tough as he likes to make out. But he does like to weed out the weak-willed before he starts. He figures anyone who would turn back because of what he says wouldn't have what it takes to make it across anyway." He paused. "And those who don't turn back will maybe take the trip a little more seriously."

Jamie said nothing else, but Fortune had the clear impression he was wondering himself whether it had been such a good idea to link up with a group of actors to cross nearly two thousand miles of mostly unsettled territory.

CHAPTER EIGHT

That night Mr. Patchett managed to find three chickens someplace in town. To everyone's surprise Jamie took over from there, plucking and dressing the birds, then doing something mysterious with some flour and spices he found in their supplies. Fortune watched him intently, wondering if her joking comments about his cooking that first day in Busted Heights were unexpectedly accurate.

They were. The chicken was tender and delectable. This was an amazement to Fortune, who found cooking an unfathomable mystery.

After dinner, though, it was her turn to shine. She took out her guitar again and began to play and sing. After a few minutes Walter went to the wagon to fetch his fiddle. (Or "violin," as he preferred to call it.) Soon the two of them were playing a lively duet that attracted their fellow wagoneers like moths to a lantern.

Before long they had an impromptu dance going full swing around them, people clapping and singing and stomping with the rhythm of their music. Two other men showed up with fiddles, someone made rhythm on a washtub, and someone else started twanging on a Jew's harp.

"Yes, sir!" cried Mr. Patchett gleefully. "It's just like your father always said, Fortune. Wherever there are people, there's a need for entertainment. We're doing the smart thing all right. Just you wait and see."

Later on, as Fortune and Walter grew tired, the party began to wind down. Singly and in pairs, their fellow travelers headed reluctantly back toward their own wagons.

The actors gathered around the fire once more, and Fortune found herself sitting between Jamie and Aaron. She felt warm, comfortable, and pleasantly tired.

The talk turned then, as it always did, to theater. For a while they discussed their plans for San Francisco, and their dream of building their own theater. At Walter's urging, Fortune got out a drawing Aaron had made to show what her father had had in mind.

"It's beautiful," said Jamie appreciatively.

"And we'll all have shares in it," said Walter proudly.

Next the conversation turned to the past. Fortune loved this part, loved listening to the three older actors tell of their experiences onstage, the crazy things that had happened to them over the years, the practical jokes they had played—or been the butt of.

Mrs. Watson told a story she had heard about the wild adventures of the famous Lola Montez, whom she greatly admired.

"I'd love to see her do that spider dance of hers someday," she added wistfully.

Mr. Patchett launched into one of his own favorite stories, the one about the time his suspenders had broken in the middle of a dramatic monologue, and he had had to finish both the speech and the ensuing love scene with one hand holding up his trousers. Fortune loved the story; no matter how many times she heard it, it made her laugh.

Eventually the conversation came around to the fire in Busted Heights, and what each of them had done that night.

"Wasn't that bad," said Walter in summation. "They had a theater fire in Richmond back in 1811 that killed seventy-one people. It just about stopped theater right across the country . . . for a while, at least. All *we* did was burn down a building or two."

"We did not!" said Fortune.

"Might as well have," said Walter philosophically. "We got kicked out of town anyway."

"It's an actor's lot," sighed Mr. Patchett. "As you'll soon find out, Mr. Jamie Halleck. Any regrets yet on tying your fortunes to a band of traveling players?"

"I've never had so much fun in my life," said Jamie. His eyes were shining, and it was obvious he meant it.

Fortune's sense of warmth and safety evaporated the next day when Jamie forced her to come face to face with how woefully underprepared they were for the journey facing them.

Greenhorns that they were, they had been totally oblivious of this fact until he suggested they take an inventory of their equipment.

"After all, we're going to be traveling close to two thousand miles, and this is our last good chance to stock up. Better to pick up some small thing you've forgotten now than to have to borrow it on the trail."

His slight smile made Fortune wonder if he harbored suspicions they might have forgotten more than "some small thing."

Yet even that hint did not prepare her for his shock when they unpacked the wagon to show him what they had. For a time he just stood in front of the pile of gear, shaking his head in amazement. "Did you think you were going to find stores all along the way?" he asked at last.

Fortune would have resented the sarcasm inherent in the question if he hadn't sounded as if he actually thought they were so inexperienced this might be the case.

Finally he heaved a deep sigh. "Well, there's nothing to do but go get what you need. You're going to get scalped for it—the storekeepers here love to make a killing on last-minute items people suddenly realize they can't live without. This may be more like a massacre. I'll do the best I can for you." He turned to Fortune. "How much money do you have?"

The question was greeted by a frozen silence. The troupe's finances were a strict secret between Walter and Fortune.

"How much do you have?" repeated Jamie.

"Not much," said Fortune tartly. "What's really necessary here, anyway?"

"Food, for one thing!" answered Jamie. "What do you think we're going to feed seven people for the next four or five months? You had no gun for hunting until I joined up with you. You have almost no staples; a few pounds of flour, a little sugar, and some coffee. That's it. Who does the cooking for this outfit anyway?"

Like children caught in a lie, they glanced at one another from the corners of their eyes. They all hated cooking.

Jamie read the message. "Well, don't worry about that. I'll handle it while we're on the road. What about tools?"

"We've got an ax!" said Mr. Patchett resentfully.

"That will be very helpful for digging you out of a mud hole," said Jamie, trying to contain his scorn.

"Look, we're not going west to settle," said Aaron. "Most of these people are going to build houses or start farms or search for gold. Of course they need tools. We're just going to act. And we still have to replace the props and costumes we lost in that fire. We don't need to spend money on a bunch of tools."

"It's true that you won't need many tools once you get there," agreed Jamie. "But you've still got to get there!"

"All right," said Fortune, stepping into her position as leader of the troupe. "You've made your point. Make a list of the things you think we can't live without, and we'll see how many we can afford."

"The only things on that list will be items you can't afford to do *without*," said Jamie sharply. It was clear he was getting angry at the troupe's response to his attempts to help them.

Walter brought Jamie a pencil and a scrap of paper. He spent the next hour working on his suggestions. When he brought the paper to Fortune, an uncomfortable silence fell over the group.

She raised her eyebrows as she examined it. "Lariats, a spade, a tent, an extra wagon tongue . . . What are we going to do with all these things?"

"The real question is what you thought you were going to do without them. If you'll give me the money, I'll go get them for you."

Aaron laughed out loud. "You must think we're really stupid. Do you expect we're going to hand our money over to a stranger and let him walk out of town with it?"

Jamie flushed with anger. "All right, go west your own way! I'll see you in California—*if* you make it!"

He turned and stalked away from the wagon.

"Wait!" cried Fortune. "Where are you going?"

"To see Abner Simpson. He offered me a scouting job last year. I imagine it's still open. If not, there are at least two other wagons I've spotted where I know people who will let me come along. Thank you for the companionship. I enjoyed being in your play. Now I'll get out of your hair!"

His eyes were flashing, his cheeks red with anger. Fortune groped for something to say as he turned and started away again.

"Wait!" she called. "I'm . . . I'm sorry for what Aaron said. I . . ." She swallowed, then spoke words that came very hard for her: "I need your help."

The look on his face softened. He smiled at her, and it was like the sudden sun that follows a storm. "Why don't you come with me?"

So she did. And it was on this afternoon that Fortune finally realized what a stroke of luck it had been for her when she agreed to let Jamie Halleck accompany the troupe to California.

To begin with, he appeared to be known by everyone who sold anything in the town of Independence. Even better, they all seemed to like him and were willing to go out of their way to help him. After catching her breath at initial prices given, Fortune would feel a sense of relief flood through her as Jamie cheerfully managed to talk the merchants into prices far lower than she would have thought possible.

"How do you know all these people?" asked Fortune, after their fourth stop.

"My father and I used to come here in the spring. There were always lots of high-paying odd jobs to pick up. It was a good way to make some honest money fast."

Fortune continued to be amazed both by how many people knew Jamie and how fond they were of him. Before the day was over he had not only done a lot of hard bargaining, he had called in a handful of old favors, in the process saving Plunkett's Players a bucketful of money.

She was smiling as they returned to camp that evening, leading a mule laden down with supplies. Though the mule was borrowed, the bacon, coffee, rice, beans, axes, ropes, and other essentials were all theirs.

When they were all unpacked, Walter bent down and hissed in her ear, "How much did all that cost?"

"About twice what I wanted," she answered. "But less than a third of what they were asking. Jamie saved us a bundle."

Walter straightened his derby, scratched his beard, and smiled down at her. "That's good. Jamie's a good boy."

Two days later they paid a ferryman to take their wagon across the Missouri River into Kansas. When they finally stood on the far bank of the river, Fortune had a sense that they had left their old world behind them and were truly facing the great unknown.

The wagons assembled.

Abner Simpson gave the call "Wagons West!"

Aaron shook the reins and urged the team into motion.

The real journey had begun at last.

CHAPTER NINE

The morning of their third day out, Fortune was sitting next to Aaron in her accustomed spot at the front of the wagon. They had traveled about thirty miles so far, and she was astonished by the vast emptiness of the land around them.

She glanced at Jamie, who was riding his horse just off to their right, and felt a surge of gratitude for all he had accomplished during the last few days.

Rolling along on the far side of Jamie was another wagon, drawn by a team of six oxen. Fortune noticed and shook her head. "I can't believe there are so many of us!" she said to Mrs. Watson, who was sitting in the wagon behind them.

She was used to traveling alone, as they had done for so long. Now when their wagon bounced its way over the ruts and bumps of the prairie, it was merely one of a crowd. Whether Fortune looked ahead, or behind, there were wagons as far as she could see, a great writhing snake of them. And each had the same goal—the golden dream of California.

Her thoughts were interrupted by a lurch and a thump, followed by a terrible cracking sound.

"Whoa!" cried Aaron, drawing up on the reins. "Whoa!"

The team jerked to a stop.

"What is it?" asked Fortune.

"We've broken an axle," said Jamie. His face was grim.

Fortune said one of those words that always made Mrs. Watson turn white and sprang off the wagon to look. It was a miserable sight. The troupe gathered around her.

"Oh, Minerva! What do we do now?" cried Mrs. Watson, wringing her hands.

"We fix it," said Jamie simply.

"I suppose you know how," snorted Aaron.

Jamie looked at him darkly. "As a matter of fact, I do. But I'll need help."

The others settled down to wait as Jamie and Aaron went to work. After a moment Jamie called Walter over and asked him to hold something. The giant gladly obliged, happy to be helping.

Watching the way Jamie took charge, Fortune realized that he was a born leader. She almost wished he had been with them from the start. She could have used someone like him.

She chased the thought from her mind. She didn't want any help. The troupe was hers and she would lead it in her own way!

Other wagons rolled by as they sat waiting. Most of them slowed, as if to offer help, but continued on when they saw the three men hard at work. Fortune was pleased. She didn't like to accept any more help than was necessary.

She reminded herself that she was accepting *Jamie's* help, then told herself it wasn't the same thing, because he was one of them. The thought shocked her. She examined it again and decided it was true. Somehow Jamie Halleck had managed to make himself a part of Plunkett's Players.

The spring sun was hot, and after a while Jamie and Aaron stripped off their shirts. Fortune couldn't help but compare their bodies as they worked: Aaron's was lean and wiry, his skin fair and smooth; Jamie's solid and muscular, with broad shoulders and a light dusting of chestnut-colored hair across his deep chest.

They're nice to look at, she said to herself, almost uncomfortable with how much she was enjoying the view. To her surprise she noticed that Mrs. Watson was also watching them intently.

She surprised herself again by thinking, *Well,*

we're both women. She let it go at that.

Her drifting thoughts were snapped back to the present by an angry shout from Jamie. "Dammit, Aaron, hold that tighter!"

Fortune was astonished by the dark look that twisted his usually cheerful face. Aaron shouted back, and for an instant she feared they might actually start to fight. Then Walter placed himself between them, his towering bulk a virtual living wall, and after a moment the tension simmering between them began to subside.

When the axle was finally fixed, it was clear to all of them that without Jamie they would have been delayed a great deal longer.

"By gum, young man, I'm sure glad you were along," said Mr. Patchett, clapping him on the shoulder. "Turns out trying to make this trip without you would have been like trying to put on *Hamlet* without—"

He cut himself off, glancing nervously at Fortune.

"Jamie is worth his weight in gold," said Aaron, his voice bitter with sarcasm. Slinging his shirt over his shoulder, he retreated to the back of the wagon.

Fortune hurried around to talk with him. "What's wrong?" she asked.

Aaron shrugged himself into his shirt. "Nothing.

I just hate wasting time. The sooner we get to California and build our theater the better."

He spun away and stalked to the front of the wagon. Springing into the seat, he shouted for the others to get ready to roll. "We've lost enough time today. Let's move!"

Fortune decided to walk for a while. Almost unconsciously, she found herself falling into place beside Jamie. Soon he slid from the saddle and walked beside her, leading his horse.

"Don't be upset with Aaron," she said after a moment. "It's hard for him to have someone do things he can't."

Jamie laughed. "I'm not upset. It's his problem, not mine. I feel sorry for him."

"Well, you needn't!" cried Fortune, her temper flaring. "There's plenty he *can* do, too! He's a fine actor, for one thing."

"I'm sure that's true," said Jamie coldly. "Sorry if I offended you."

The conversation was hopeless after that. In a little while she drifted over to walk beside Walter, who was always happy to have her company. He entertained her with a story about his childhood in England and soon lifted her out of her dark mood.

When she rejoined Aaron at the head of the wagon, he was silent for a long time. When he finally spoke, it was to ask in a malicious tone, "Well, did you tell our Jamie how proud you were of him?"

"Oh, be quiet and drive," she snapped.

Then she crossed her arms and said nothing else for the rest of the day. It wasn't worth the risk.

The evening was better, for after they had cleaned up from their supper, Walter and Fortune hauled out their instruments, which attracted several of their fellow travelers. Fortune noticed one in particular, a quick, bright-eyed girl who stayed at the edge of the firelight but looked at her with a kind of hunger that she had come to recognize long ago. The girl was struck by the glamour and strangeness of a troupe of players.

The gathering broke up when Abner Simpson came striding by and reminded everyone that he expected them to be ready to roll early the next morning.

"I'm beginning to hate that man," said Fortune when he had disappeared into the darkness.

"I think he's very handsome," said Mrs. Watson.

"I'll tell you the one I hate," said Edmund. "It's the one who blows the bugle."

The chorus of groans from the others indicated that Edmund had managed to say something they all agreed with, a rarity for him. The troupe was used to both late nights and late mornings, and the discipline of the wagon train, which required every-one to rise at six, was difficult for them. Only Jamie was unaffected by it, since, as he said, he was used to his mother waking him for his day's chores at five.

"I'm enjoying the extra hour's sleep!" he had said with a grin that only made the others feel even more sour about their schedule.

Since no one wanted to cook in the morning, they tended to start their days with bread and coffee left from the night before. The cold coffee in particular tasted vile. So Fortune was delighted when she woke the morning of the fourth day to the smell of fresh-brewing coffee.

"Howdy," said Jamie when she stepped from the wagon. "Woke up on my old schedule and figured I might as well make myself useful."

"Seems to be a habit of yours," she said.

It was a good start to a good day. About halfway through the morning, when Fortune was walking beside the wagon, the girl she had noticed the night before dropped back to walk beside her. When Fortune greeted her, she smiled shyly, but didn't say anything. Indeed they walked in silence for such a long period that Fortune began to wonder if the girl was a mute. Finally she asked the girl's name.

"Rebecca Hyatt," she replied, looking up shyly from under the brim of her sunbonnet. "But people call me Becky. And you're Fortune, right?"

Fortune smiled. "That's right."

"My pa saw you once," said Becky. "When he was in Charleston on business. He said you were very good."

"Give your pa my thanks," said Fortune.

"Is it wonderful?" asked Becky suddenly. "Being an actress, I mean? I think it would be wonderful." She gasped at her own boldness. "My ma would skin me alive if I ever said that in front of her! She says actors are—" She broke off and began to blush furiously. "Never mind what she thinks. *I* think it must be wonderful."

Fortune didn't answer right away. She didn't think much about whether it was wonderful to be an actress or not. She had never known anything else. But the longing in this girl's voice, like the longing that Jamie had shown to join the troupe, made her remember that other people saw it differently.

"It's hard work," said Fortune at last. "And I do get tired of all the traveling." She stopped, looked around, and laughed. It was absurd to complain about traveling to a fellow member of the wagon train. They were all travelers now, and would be for months to come.

CHAPTER TEN

Jamie stood in front of the group holding a brown, crusty item about the size of a dinner plate. "See this? I need you to get some more of them for me."

"What is it?" asked Fortune.

"A buffalo chip."

She looked at him in astonishment. "What are you talking about?"

"Supper."

"Oh, Minerva!" cried Mrs. Watson. "I knew it would come to this sooner or later. Are we out of food already?"

Jamie laughed. "We're not going to eat them. I'm going to cook with them. Unless one of you wants to do that instead—or can think of something better to make a fire with."

Fortune looked around. The land rolled on in all directions without a tree in sight. Even so, she wondered if Jamie was playing some sort of joke on them—revenge, perhaps, for the way Aaron and Edmund had tormented him during his first rehearsal back in Bevins.

As if to confirm that he was serious, she saw Becky Hyatt coming back to her family's camp with an apron full of the very things that Jamie was asking them to gather.

So out they went to hunt for buffalo chips. As she pried the first one out of the grass, Fortune congratulated herself on living the glamorous life of an actress.

It was enough to make her wish she had learned how to cook.

The train had its first accident the next day, when a little boy fell beneath the wheels of his family's wagon. His cries of pain were horrible to hear. Even more horrible was the sudden silence that fell late in the afternoon.

Some of the men buried the boy that night. They had seen other graves along the way. They would pass hundreds more before the journey was over.

Though Fortune expected the tragedy to delay the trip, the next morning Abner Simpson headed them on their way again. Whatever grieving the boy's family needed to do would have to be done while traveling. Sorrow alone, no matter how deep, was not a sufficient reason to delay the journey.

"It's not decent," said Fortune.

Becky Hyatt was walking beside her. To her surprise, the girl took a grimly practical position: "Decent or not, we can't wait," she said. "My pa says if we stop every time someone dies, we'll probably end up freezing in the mountains."

Mrs. Watson, too, had surprised Fortune by taking the boy's mother under her wing. She almost disappeared from the troupe's wagon for the next several days, spending all her time providing companionship and support for the grieving woman.

It took twenty days in all for the wagon train to cover the nearly three hundred miles to Fort Kearny, the first settlement of any size after the beginning of their journey.

The fort was a dismal place, but at least they were able to buy a few supplies that they needed, including some flour and some coffee.

Fortune was fascinated by the record the commandant had made of the people who had passed the fort on the westward trip—nearly fifty thousand people, a good third of them women and children.

*　*　*

On a cool, pleasant night in mid-May they camped near the Platte River. Fortune remembered one of the letters her father had read her from the newspaper, in which one of the earlier travelers had described the river as "a mile wide and an inch deep."

That was an exaggeration, of course—though not much of one, Fortune thought as she stood at the water's edge. She watched the water rolling on, and wished that she could move as easily. She was beginning to think that the journey—and the continent—were endless.

She came back to the camp to find the men debating the truth of Abner Simpson's claim that the Indians they had seen the day before sometimes ate grasshoppers.

Though Fortune was exhausted, sleep wouldn't come. As she lay in the narrow wagon beside the snoring Mrs. Watson, a million thoughts were racing through her mind, most of them having to do with Jamie and Aaron.

Mrs. Watson gave a loud snort and rolled over, tossing an arm across Fortune's shoulders.

"That does it!" she muttered. "I've got to get out of here!"

Scrambling to her feet, she wrapped a blanket around her shoulders, then climbed out of the wagon. When she turned and looked up, she caught her breath in wonder. The huge sky, so much bigger than she was used to back East, was blazing with stars. The vastness of it made her feel tiny, insignificant.

She turned in a slow circle, trying to take it all in. To the west, in the direction they were heading, a bar of darkness covered the stars in the lower quarter of the sky. Distant thunder rumbled, so softly she could barely hear it above the soft thrum of the insects. The wind from the west carried the sweet scent of the prairie in bloom.

I want someone to share this with, she thought desperately. *It's too beautiful for just one person.*

Several wagons away she could hear some of the men hooting and shouting. She frowned. It was a sound she associated with saloons and drinking, and it made her think of her father's death. The raucousness seemed a scar on the serene beauty of the night.

Moving quietly, she walked away from the shouting, heading for where Romeo, Juliet, and the rest of the team were tethered. The horses were grazing in a slow, lazy fashion. Other horses were nearby. Fortune enjoyed the sound they made tearing up the tender spring grass, the musky smell of their bodies.

"Hi, Romeo," she said softly. "Hello there, Juliet."

The gelding raised his head and whickered. Juliet, however, continued to eat, completely ignoring Fortune's arrival.

"Oh, don't be so uppity," she said to the mare. At the same time she began scratching Romeo behind the ears. As soon as Juliet noticed the attention Romeo was getting, she crossed to join them.

Thunder rumbled, closer now than when she had left the wagon.

"Must be nice being a horse," Fortune said to Romeo, pointedly ignoring Juliet. "Less to worry about."

Juliet blew out a gust of air, causing her lips to flap.

Fortune laughed. "Well, there's no need to be rude if you don't agree! I just meant it seems as if it would be easy to have so many of your decisions made for you. You don't have to worry about which way you're going, or who you're going with. That's all taken care of."

"It does make life easier, doesn't it?" asked a husky voice behind her.

Fortune spun around. "Aaron!"

"Couldn't sleep?" he asked. His words were oddly slurred, and Fortune's delight at seeing him faded as she found herself trying to fight down the feeling that she heard something menacing in his voice.

"Just sore from walking all day," she said, forcing a laugh.

"And not even a little bit lonely?"

He stepped closer. His breath was rank with the smell of cheap liquor, and Fortune realized that he had been part of the wild group she had heard back at the wagons. "Not lonely at all," she lied. "I like the solitude."

"'S funny," said Aaron. "Beautiful night like this, you'd think a . . . a pretty girl standing out here by herself would just be longing for someone to share it with."

"I was looking at the stars."

Aaron glanced up. The sky was darkening as the cloud bank moved in from the west, but overhead, and to the east, the stars were still as brilliant as ever. "They're beautiful," he said, taking another step closer. "Just like you."

"But I'm getting cold now," said Fortune. "I think I'll go back to the wagon."

Aaron took her arm. "Stay a while," he said softly. "Maybe you don't mind being alone, but I don't like it. I want some company. I'm lonely, Fortune."

He sounded on the verge of tears. But she had heard drunks cry before, and the sound did not raise sympathy in her. "I really have to get back," she said, shaking her arm free of his grip. "Mrs.

Watson might wake up. She'll be worried if I'm not there."

"Don't worry about her. She sleeps like a log." He took her arm again and pulled her around so they were face to face.

Fortune was glad that it was too dark to see him clearly—or for him to see her. She felt as if she were being torn in half. She had yearned so long for him to show her some attention, some affection. Yet the moment had been ruined by his foolish drunkenness.

He pulled her closer, slipping his arms around her.

"Don't," said Fortune, turning her head to avoid the smell of the liquor. "Aaron, *don't!*"

"Listen to me." His voice was desperate, his eyes flashing. "No. Don't listen. Words are . . . stupid. They cut you." Tightening his arms, he drew her toward him, moving his lips toward hers.

Fortune struggled to break free of his grip.

"Hold still!" said Aaron roughly. "You're such a . . . tease, bouncing back and forth between Jamie and me. I get sick of . . . I want to . . . they said . . ."

He stopped talking and tried to kiss her. Though part of her longed to respond, she was revolted by the smell of the alcohol. Turning her face away, she hissed, "Let go of me!"

When he didn't relax his grip, she tried to tear herself from his arms. "Aaron, *let go!*" she shouted. With a burst of unsuspected strength, she finally managed to wrench one arm free. When she did, she slapped his face so hard it made her hand sting.

Romeo, startled by the sudden movement, shied away from them. Juliet whinnied nervously.

Aaron gasped in astonishment. He put his hand to his mouth, which was bleeding. He stared at her for a moment, then turned and stumbled into the darkness. She heard him start to vomit, and the sound made her own stomach twist with nausea. But her contempt for his drunkenness was tempered by memories of her father's occasional "nights out," and she wondered if she should try to help him back to the wagon.

After a moment she followed his moans into the darkness. He was on his knees, shaking.

"I'm sorry," he whispered. "Sorry sorry sorry. It was a mistake. I can't . . . they don't understand. My fault, my fault . . ."

Putting his head in his hands he began to weep.

Fortune reached down to help him to his feet. "Come on. We'd better get back to the wagon before this storm hits."

That turned out to be impossible. They hadn't

gone ten feet before the rain began to fall with a force that astonished Fortune, pounding against her so hard that it hurt. Nothing she had read of the fierce prairie storms had prepared her for the reality of this one. Lightning cascaded across the sky like the wrath of the gods made real. The thunder that accompanied it seemed to shake the earth itself.

When a bolt of lightning sizzled down terrifyingly close to them, Aaron threw himself to the ground and covered his head, whimpering in distress. Fortune looked at him in disgust. It was all she could do to keep herself from kicking him and shouting, "Get up, you fool!"

She stopped, frozen, realizing that she had seen her mother do that to her father once.

A wave of sickness washed over her, and she fell to her knees herself. The rain continued to pound against them. She pushed the horrifying memory away. Using her hands, she found Aaron's shoulders, then his head. Putting her mouth close to his ear, she shouted, "Aaron! Aaron, get up and come with me. We have to get back to the wagon."

It wasn't until she stood and began to pull at him that he finally staggered to his feet again.

The darkness and the pounding rain made it impossible to see more than a few inches ahead.

They tripped and stumbled along, and it was only by luck that they managed to find their way back to the campsite rather than go wandering off across the prairie.

She left Aaron at the door of the men's tent. She was too tired and filled with despair to be amused by the cries of dismay from the others when he stumbled, soggy and dripping, into their midst.

Splashing through the puddles, she climbed over the back of the wagon. It was wet in there, too, the painted cloth cover insufficient to withstand the full fury of the storm.

Even so, it was home—or as much of a home as she had at the moment. The sound of Mrs. Watson's snoring, so annoying such a short time before, suddenly seemed oddly comforting.

Stripping off her soaked things, Fortune climbed into her makeshift bed. Pressing her face to her blanket so that Mrs. Watson would not hear, she cried herself to sleep.

CHAPTER ELEVEN

It was three days before either of them spoke of what had happened. Fortune was riding beside Aaron at the front of the wagon—something she had avoided entirely the previous two days—when he said, "About the other night . . ."

"I don't want to talk about it!"

Aaron nodded, and fell silent. Fortune glanced at him from the corner of her eye. He was staring straight ahead, his jaw set. A moment later he tried again. "Listen. I just want to say I'm sorry. It was a stupid thing to do."

She relaxed a little. "I'm sorry I got so mad," she said.

He shook his head. "You had every right."

They rode in silence for another moment, then he reached for her hand. She let him take it. Yet the gesture didn't make her nearly as happy as she wanted it to. Her feelings for him, once so clear, were now as muddy and churned as the road beneath them.

Turning her head, Fortune began to study the vast prairie that stretched away on all sides of them. As always, she was amazed at the flowers, sweeps of red, orange, and yellow that looked like schools of multicolored fishes swimming through an ocean of grass. Life seemed to pulse around her—the hawks that circled overhead, the insects that buzzed and swarmed over the grasses. She knew there was more life, too, life she was less apt to see, like the coyotes that sometimes prowled the edges of their camp at night, the rattlesnakes she had been warned against, the red deer the men sometimes shot and carried back to camp.

She had been revolted the first time she saw Jamie clean and gut a deer; it was the only time in her life that she had been forced to come face to face with the reality of the meat she ate.

Her squeamishness had evoked some teasing from Edmund and Aaron, and also left her thinking about some of the other women she had met on the journey—women like Becky Hyatt's mother, who had been killing and cleaning animals since she was a child.

Eventually Fortune slipped her hand from Aaron's and scrambled back into the wagon to talk to Mrs. Watson.

*   *   *

The red-haired woman sat serenely on a chair she had wedged between two chests, looking like a queen in exile. She had a book in one hand and was quietly turning the pages, as if the bounce and bump of the wagon had no effect on her at all.

Fortune sat on the rounded top of one of the chests next to her and waited for Mrs. Watson to notice her. When it became clear that she was so absorbed in her book that she wasn't going to, Fortune asked loudly, "What are you reading?"

"Why, Fortune!" Mrs. Watson seemed genuinely pleased to see her. She closed her book and looked at the cover. "It's called *Frankenstein,*" she said with a shudder. "Most gruesome thing I ever read. Gives me the shivers. Written by a young woman not much older than you, believe it or not. It's about a scientist who builds a new man out of the parts of dead people!"

Fortune blinked in astonishment at such a revolting idea. "If it's so horrible, why are you reading it?" She looked at the book as if it might bite her.

"Oh, I *love* to have the shivers. Besides, it's how I get away from all this bouncing and jouncing. I can pretend I'm not here at all."

As if on cue, the wagon rolled over another bump, sending both passengers an inch or two off their seats. Mrs. Watson put her hand against her back and groaned. "Sometimes I think that even if I do live to see California, my spine will have been ground to powder by the time we get there."

"Maybe you should walk for a while, as the others do," suggested Fortune.

"The sun would be devastating for my complexion, chicken. I don't know how you can stand it out there yourself. If you must walk, I wish you would stop taking off your bonnet. You're doing terrible things to your skin."

"I'm sure," said Fortune. "Even so, I prefer it to being cooped up in here."

She paused, uncertain how to talk about what was on her mind, afraid Mrs. Watson would laugh. She wasn't even sure she *should* talk about it.

Mrs. Watson looked at her closely. "Are you all right, chickadee?"

"What? Oh, certainly. Only . . . Mrs. Watson, did you ever have . . . man trouble?"

She did laugh, but it was a friendly, confiding laugh. "What woman hasn't? It's the curse of our sex. Also the blessing. What's bothering you? Aaron, or Jamie? Not Edmund, I hope. Silly little peacock."

Fortune made a face. "Not Edmund! Aaron, mostly. The other night . . ."

She fell silent, unable to tell the story.

Mrs. Watson looked at her, but said nothing.

The wagon bounced and bumped along.

Finally Fortune spoke again. Hesitantly at first, then overcome by memory and anger and sorrow, she poured out her story. She included Aaron's apology, but didn't mention the way he had just taken her hand.

Mrs. Watson shook her head, and Fortune could tell that she was delighted to be consulted in this matter. "There, there, love. Men do that sort of thing every once in a while. At least, a lot of them do. The thing to ask yourself is, does it happen all the time, or was it just a mistake? We all do make mistakes, chicken—even us women. Sometimes we even mistake strong feelings for love."

"What do you mean?" asked Fortune suspiciously.

Mrs. Watson shrugged. "You need to be on your guard, Fortune. Right now you have to figure you're sort of like a mouse in a roomful of hungry cats. You may not be much, but you're the best thing around."

"Well, thank you very much!"

"Don't be a goose. I didn't mean it like that. Anyway, what a smart mouse would do is play the cats off against each other. As long as they're fighting over the mouse, they won't be trying to catch it."

Fortune thought for a moment. Finally, timidly, she asked, "What if the mouse *wants* to get caught?"

Mrs. Watson smiled. "Ah, now that's different. First you have to choose your cat."

Choosing to ignore the implication of that statement, Fortune said nothing for a while. She began to study Mrs. Watson's face and realized that her expression wasn't merely serious; it was almost mournful.

Yet there was a veil behind her eyes, as if she were shutting out the world—or holding something away from it. Prompted by something she didn't quite understand, Fortune asked, "Did you ever have a dream, Mrs. Watson?"

"Once," she replied, her voice soft and husky. "For a while."

"What happened?"

Mrs. Watson's eyes grew dark, and her face seemed to close in on itself, shutting Fortune out somehow. "It's a long story, dear," she whispered, "and I'd really rather not talk about it." She paused, and stared past Fortune at the light filtering through the wagon cover. Suddenly she straightened her spine and said, almost fiercely, "But I will tell you one thing—something I know, as sure as I know the sun will rise tomorrow morning. Once you figure out what you want, you're a fool if you don't fight for it with all your heart and soul." She paused. The mask of cheerfulness she usually wore returned. The memory, whatever it was, had been pushed back into hiding.

"One more thing, Fortune."

"Yes?"

Mrs. Watson picked up her book. "Until you do know what you want, you're a fool if you don't have some fun finding out." She paused, then added, "The thing about cats is, they can't control themselves. Twitch something in front of them the right way and they'll dive for it, whether they want it or not. It makes them a lot of fun to play with."

She returned to *Frankenstein*. The talk was over.

Fortune started for the front of the wagon, then decided to climb through the back instead and walk for a while.

The prairie stretched into the distance. Though Fortune could see nothing that really qualified as a hill, certainly nothing that blocked the seemingly endless view of grass, the land was not as flat as she had been warned—as she could tell by the burning in her calves that came from walking up and down the rolling landscape.

After a while Jamie slid off Dolly, tied her to the back of the wagon, and fell into step beside Fortune. They walked in silence for several minutes. Finally he said, "That was some storm the other night."

Fortune looked at him suspiciously, wondering if he was aware of what had happened.

"I don't like the wind," she said at last. "It blows so hard out here."

"Oh, that wind wasn't much," said Jamie. "Last year the wind blew so hard in Busted Heights that one day I watched one of our chickens lay the same egg four times."

Fortune snorted.

"Her sister was smarter, though," continued Jamie, as if he had not heard. "She just turned around and opened her mouth and—*Pop! Pop! Pop!*—laid five eggs in three minutes. Most amazing thing I ever saw."

"Do you always talk such nonsense?" asked Fortune, trying not to show how amused she was.

He shrugged. "I can be serious if you want." He waited a moment. Then, as if to prove the statement, he looked at her and said, "Are you in love with Aaron?"

Fortune let out a little gasp. She was not used to such a blunt approach.

Not as surprising, but more distressing, was the fact that she had no idea what the answer was. A week earlier she would have said yes without even thinking about it. Now she realized she could think about it all day and not be sure.

Jamie repeated the question. His voice was gentle, but insistent.

She looked at him closely. His brown eyes seemed larger than ever; they had a soft quality, a vulnerability, that reminded her of a child who has skinned a knee. Yet they held something else, too; something hidden. She had the sudden feeling she could know him for a lifetime yet never know everything about him.

"I don't know," she said. Then added, a little peevishly, "And it's none of your business if I am anyway!"

He nodded. "That's true. On the other hand, I'm glad you don't know."

Fortune wasn't sure if she was being laughed at. Every time she talked to him, she realized how wrong she had been in her initial perception of him as "just" a small-town boy.

"Have *you* ever been in love?" she asked casually.

"Once or twice. Of course, there weren't that many people to fall in love with in Busted Heights. I did have a dog I was crazy about once. . . ."

She let out a hearty laugh, half in amusement, half to break the tension. "You're cracked."

"I thought that was a requirement for anyone who wanted to be an actor."

"It probably should be," she said, half-seriously.

He bent and picked one of the purple flowers

that Becky Hyatt had told her was called a shooting star. "A flower for milady!" he said triumphantly, holding it out to her.

Uncertain of what to say, Fortune took the blossom from his hand. Looking down at the flower, she caressed it with her fingertip. The petals were soft and smooth, their colors more shaded and varied than she had realized at first glance.

The wagon creaked and rumbled beside them. The sun was warm but gentle, the air sweet with new growth.

Jamie took the flower from her hand. She was still looking away as he threaded it through her hair, over one ear.

She turned to him and smiled. The sunlight burnished his chestnut hair, touching it with bronze and gold. She had an almost irresistible urge to touch it, to run her fingers through it.

Careful, Fortune Plunkett. Don't let yourself get carried away!

"What happened to your father?" asked Jamie, as if sensing her discomfort, her need to change the subject.

"He died. Of pneumonia."

"I'm sorry. Does it bother you to talk about it?"

"No. Yes." She turned her face away again. "I don't know."

She had a sudden vision of her father, tall and

handsome, standing on the stage, commanding an audience, overwhelming them with the power and beauty of his voice.

"Are you all right?" asked Jamie.

She took a deep breath, realized that she had stopped walking. "I think so." She paused. "Do you want to know how it happened?"

"Only if you want to tell me."

She walked in silence for several minutes. She hadn't spoken with anyone about her father's death. It was too personal, too painful, too recent. And yet somehow she felt she could trust Jamie to listen without intruding. She felt a sudden need to empty herself of the memory.

"Last year, around Christmastime, we had a fantastically successful week—a new town every night, and a full house in each one of them. You don't get a lot of weeks like that. We were staying in a place called Burke's Crossing. A little river ran through the center of the town."

She shivered. "On Friday night Papa, Walter, Aaron, and Mr. Patchett went to a tavern after the show, to celebrate our good luck." She paused again. "Papa had too much to drink."

Her voice had a defensive edge. "He didn't do that very often, you know. It just happened that night."

"I believe you."

She searched his face. Satisfied with what she saw, she went on. "Anyway, they were coming back to the boardinghouse—it was a lot like your mother's place, actually—and when they stepped onto the bridge it reminded Papa of a stage. So he decided to make a speech—one of the big monologues from *Hamlet*. After he got rolling, he climbed up onto the railing."

She smiled ruefully. "Papa was always very dramatic when he was drunk. Anyway, he finished the speech with a flourish, took a bow . . . and fell into the river."

The day seemed to have lost its warmth. She rubbed her hands together nervously. "They fished him out before he could drown. But he caught pneumonia. That was what killed him."

Suddenly Jamie seemed far away, and she was back in the little room where her father lay dying. She could see the weak sunlight filtering through a dirty window, smell again the closed, moist sickroom odor. Mr. Patchett was standing at the foot of the bed. Walter was in the corner, filling it with his presence, staring down at her mournfully as if it were all his fault for not somehow preventing the tragedy.

Her father took her hand. He started to speak, but his voice was weak, and she had to lean close to hear.

"I'm not going to make it, sweetheart."

Her throat knotted. Unable to speak, she squeezed his fingers tightly. Though she wanted to deny it, she knew he was right.

"Don't give up the dream," he said fiercely. "Take the troupe to California. Keep them together. Build our theater." He coughed, his body racked by the spasms. After a moment the spell subsided. "Don't let Plunkett's Players fall apart, Fortune. This journey that we've started on is the right one, darling. Promise me that you will finish it."

And though the trip had been his dream and not hers, she had bent close, kissed his forehead, and said, "I will."

"Those were the last words he ever spoke to me," she whispered. "He died in his sleep that night. I was sitting beside him . . . but I was asleep, too."

"Pardon me?" said Jamie.

She shook herself out of her reverie. "Nothing." She looked toward the hills looming in the distance. "I was talking to myself."

CHAPTER TWELVE

The journey continued. As they traveled farther west, away from all that she had known,
Fortune began to feel both lonely and more free.
Though she missed the world she had known, at
the same time she—and, she could sense, the
other women in the train as well—began to shed
some of the strictures that tied women down back
East, the things that said, "This a woman must do;
this she must not."

Not that she had paid as much attention to
those rules as most women to begin with; a life in
the theater had already set her on the outskirts of
polite society. But on a trip like this, survival came
before "must" and "must not," and she could feel
the other women in the train begin to accept her
and Mrs. Watson in a way she was not used to.

Some days the train made fifteen or twenty
miles. Others they spent from sunrise to sunset

simply trying to get all the wagons across a river.

Twice they had to cross long stretches that held no water at all. These were dangerous passages, and many of the animals did not survive the second one. Fortune herself was nearly delirious with thirst by the time they reached the shallow river they had been aiming for. They had to filter the dark, muddy water through a cloth before they could drink it. Brown and slightly acrid, it was still the most delicious thing she had ever tasted.

Though their fellow travelers had seemed somewhat wary of the actors when the journey started, shared adversity began to break down those barriers. The troupe made friends with others in the train, Becky Hyatt's family in particular.

Fortune even came to have a grudging respect for Abner Simpson—not only for his knowledge of the trail, but also for his ability to spin out tall tales, a skill that made him in some ways like a one-man theater.

By the time they entered the mountains, two of the women in the wagon train had given birth. Alas, one of the babies had died after less than a day. Its grave joined the hundreds of others that lined the trail, and the parents said nothing more about it.

Some days they had passed as many as fifteen or twenty such graves, most of them marked by simple wooden crosses. The majority of them, according to Mr. Hyatt, were victims of cholera, which occasionally swept through a wagon train with terrible suddenness, wiping out travelers by the dozen.

Fortune heard much talk of the disease—more than she cared to, really—and by the time they came upon a lone child whose family had been cut down by it, she knew that the cholera's onset was swift and vicious; that vomiting and diarrhea robbed the body of fluid, making dehydration a great danger; that of those who contracted it, far more died than recovered.

The child, a little girl of about six, was half dead with weeping herself. She was taken in by the family who had lost their boy in the wagon accident.

Amidst these life-and-death struggles, Fortune sometimes saw her own problems as small indeed. Yet they were vexing still, for she had never been so confused in her life. After his apology for his behavior on the night of the storm, Aaron seemed to relax toward her, acting almost as if he now assumed that they were a couple. This both surprised and distressed her, for she was no longer as certain as she had once been of her own feelings about him.

Yet, as had always been the way with them, they never discussed the matter. Fortune wondered why it was that she could so easily speak other people's lines on the stage, but found it so difficult to say what was in her own heart.

Jamie's presence only complicated things, since she suspected that part of Aaron's new warmth was in response to what he saw as competition. Part of her was amused by this, another part of her was angry. She felt that it should have happened before, without the spur of Jamie's presence.

"Well, you never know what you have until you're in danger of losing it," explained Mrs. Watson, during one of what had become their daily conversations in the wagon. "Besides, Jamie is only part of the change."

Some of the cookware rattled as the wagon started up a steep hill, and Mrs. Watson paused to adjust the way she was sitting. "The thing is, Fortune, you've started to blossom—sort of like a caterpillar," she added, blithely mixing her metaphors.

"What do you mean?"

"Aaron is a very sophisticated young man, chicken. When he first met you, I daresay you were a bit of a tomboy for the likes of him. And certainly you were too young for him."

145

Fortune started to protest, but Mrs. Watson spoke on over her words. "When you took over the troupe last December you started to change—to grow up." She looked at Fortune appraisingly. "By a lucky chance that seems to have coincided with what your body was ready to do."

Fortune knew this was true. She had been pleasantly aware of how her body was rounding out, the way her breasts had begun to swell, her waist to taper. The problem was she had had so much to do since responsibility for the troupe fell on her shoulders that she had not had time to really understand these changes.

Thinking about that now gave her a sharp pang of longing for her mother. She was about to speak again when the wagon slid to the right. Fortune and Mrs. Watson grabbed at the sides to keep from being thrown to the floor. They could hear Aaron yelling. The wagon rolled forward, and with a jolt they were level again.

"Is that 'blossoming' so important to a man?" asked Fortune, once they had recovered from being jounced around.

Mrs. Watson laughed. "Let's just say it doesn't hurt, ducky."

Fortune laughed too. It felt good. The last weeks had been difficult, and there hadn't been enough reason to laugh. In addition to everything

146

else, the constant tension between Jamie and Aaron had begun to get on her nerves.

Yet at the same time she had enjoyed flirting with them, watching the way they reacted to each other, and to her.

She had sensed a feeling of disapproval from Mr. Patchett. But that was only natural. As her father's best friend, he probably wanted her to stay a little girl forever. She had begun to realize that in his heart her father had felt that way.

She didn't really blame him. She figured if she ever had a baby, she would want to keep it with her forever. She wondered if it bothered Mrs. Watson not to have any children.

The next afternoon Fortune was walking beside Mr. Patchett, who was telling her a long story about a time when he was a little boy and had been introduced to Thomas Jefferson. They were nearing the crest of a trail section that led over a low mountain. The trail hugged the side of the mountain as tightly as possible with a drop to the left so severe it was frightening.

"I tell you, Jefferson should have been an actor!" concluded Mr. Patchett triumphantly. "He would have been a real star!"

Fortune was wondering if Mr. Patchett would be insulted if she suggested that what Jefferson had done was probably more important than acting when she heard a shout from Aaron. It was followed by a series of terrified whinnies from the horses. Looking ahead, she saw that the wagon had moved too close to the edge of the trail and one wheel had gone over. Now the whole wagon was tipped precariously over the steep drop.

"Mrs. Watson is in there!" cried Fortune, grabbing Mr. Patchett by the arm.

They ran for the wagon, as did Edmund and Walter, who had been walking behind them. Aaron remained in place, shouting at the horses, trying to get them to pull the wagon back on to the trail.

Stationing themselves at the wheels, the players pressed their hands to the spokes and tried to roll the wagon back up. It wouldn't budge. Indeed, it seemed to be tipping farther over.

"What's happening?" cried Mrs. Watson, her voice tinged with hysteria. "What is going on out there?"

"We've got a problem with the wagon!" shouted Fortune. "You'd better get out."

"Oh, Minerva," moaned Mrs. Watson. Fortune could hear her start to move to the front of the wagon. At the same time Aaron urged the horses into another attempt to pull the wheel over the lip of the cliff, which only caused the wagon to tip farther sideways. Walter clutched the side of the wagon, roaring at it as if he could keep it on the trail by sheer rage. Mrs. Watson's scream was nearly drowned in the clatter of falling objects.

"Are you all right?" shouted Fortune.

No answer.

"Mrs. Watson, are you all right?"

When there was still no answer Fortune said, "I'm going in after her."

"You can't do that!" cried Mr. Patchett. He grabbed her arm to hold her back. "Fortune, that wagon could go over at any minute."

"All the more reason to get Mrs. Watson out now!" snapped Fortune.

The disagreement was interrupted by the arrival of Jamie, who had been riding ahead of the group. He sprang from his saddle and hurried to the wagon. Other travelers were approaching as well, the ones who had been following them on the trail, and Becky Hyatt's father, Frank, who had been traveling just ahead of them.

"Don't look good," said Mr. Hyatt glumly.

Fortune bit back a sharp comment. "What can we do?" she asked.

Jamie went to the edge of the trail. Dropping to his hands and knees, he studied the terrain. "Nowhere down there for us to stand and try to push it back up. Might be best if we put a man at the head of each horse and try to pull it back slowly."

As he spoke Aaron tried yet again to get the horses to pull the wagon over the lip of the trail. The only result was that the wagon tipped even farther to its side.

"Stop!" cried Jamie. "You're going to lose it altogether if you're not careful!"

Aaron threw him a black look, but did not try to lash the horses forward again.

"Thing is, it might go over, even if we go slow," said Mr. Hyatt.

"Chance we have to take," said Jamie simply. "Though maybe we should try to get as much of our equipment and supplies out as we can."

"I don't think that's a good idea," said Mr. Hyatt. "You get messing around in there, and it's apt to go over with you."

"All right, then we'll lead the horses and take our chances." He started toward the team.

"Not yet!" cried Fortune. "Mrs. Watson is still in there! I think she's unconscious."

Jamie's face turned pale. "We have to get her out before we try anything else." He changed course, starting back toward the wagon.

"What are you going to do?" asked Fortune.

"Go in after her."

"I think I'd better do it," said Fortune.

Mr. Patchett looked at her in horror. "Are you out of your mind?"

It was all Fortune could do to keep from stamping her foot in frustration. "Of course not. Are you? What do you think is going to happen when someone goes into that wagon? It's going to tip more, that's what! So who do we send in? The lightest person we have, that's who! Which happens to be me, not this big horse. Sorry, Jamie—you know what I mean."

"Yeah, I know. But I don't like it much."

"Well, you don't have much choice. We're not just talking about who takes the risk. We're talking about Mrs. Watson's life. Lighter is safer. I'm it."

She started purposefully toward the wagon.

"Wait!" said Jamie.

"Don't try to stop me!"

"I'm not trying to stop you; I'm trying to get you to do this the smart way. You're right—you should be the one to go in. But what are you going to do once you're in there?"

Fortune paused. She hadn't thought that far ahead.

"Mr. Hyatt, can you get us a rope?" asked Jamie.

"Peter, fetch a rope," said Mr. Hyatt to his son, who was among the growing crowd watching the situation.

"Now what I suggest is that as many of us as can fit line up along this side of the wagon when Fortune goes in," said Jamie. "Even if we can't haul it back up on the trail, we might be able to keep it from going over."

Fortune nodded. Her initial determination had given way to a fearful realization of what she was actually about to do, and she wanted all the help she could get.

When Peter Hyatt returned with the rope, his father tied a loop in the end. "See if you can get your friend into that," he said, handing the loop to Fortune and keeping the other end of the rope himself. "Then maybe we can haul her out."

Fortune started toward the tottering wagon.

"You hold on to it, too!" said Jamie. "Aaron, you better climb on down. Maybe you should take the head of the team, try to keep them calm."

Without speaking, Aaron followed Jamie's suggestion.

Fortune waited until the men had stationed themselves on either side of Walter, who had not let go of the wagon during all this. Jamie nodded to Fortune. "Be careful," he said solemnly.

The look in his eyes tightened the knot of fear that had begun to grow in her stomach. Taking a deep breath, she began to climb up the side. She went slowly, trying not to make any sudden movements. Careful as she was, the dirt under the rear wheel that was still on the trail gave way a little. The men shouted and tightened their grip on the wagon as it tipped another inch or two to the side.

When Fortune pulled herself up far enough to look inside, her heart sank. Almost everything had slid to the left, with the bulk of it toward the back. No wonder they were having such a hard time holding it, much less getting it back onto the trail.

At first she couldn't see Mrs. Watson at all. Finally she spotted her red hair and realized that the woman was half buried under the contents of a trunk that had broken loose.

Clutching the rope, she climbed in.

The wagon shifted again, and she could hear the shouts of the men as they tried to hold it. She slipped and fell sideways, striking her head on a shovel. Blood poured down her face.

Somewhere far away Aaron was cursing. Bracing herself against the side of the wagon, Fortune pulled herself up. For the first time she looked out the back. She had to fight to keep from shouting in terror. Behind them yawned a great void—a drop into sheer emptiness. She had known it was there, of course, but knowing it and facing it as she did now were two different things.

Slowly, carefully, she made her way down toward Mrs. Watson. The wagon shifted and tipped another couple of times as she moved, but only slightly. Even so, Fortune's heart seemed to be trying to pound its way out of her chest.

"Mrs. Watson," she said, reaching out to take the older woman's arm. "Mrs. Watson, can you hear me?"

Suddenly Mrs. Watson reached up and clutched Fortune's hand with a grip that was like an eagle's talons. "Don't let me fall," she whispered. "Please don't let me fall, Fortune!"

Fortune put her other hand on Mrs. Watson's hair. "It will be all right," she replied fiercely. "I'll get us out of here. We're going to California, remember?"

As she spoke, she tried to position herself so that she could get the rope around Mrs. Watson's shoulders. The movement caused the wagon to shudder and tip farther to the side. For a dizzying moment Fortune saw a whirl of clouds and treetops through the opening in the back of the wagon. She was afraid she was going to be sick.

"Fortune, don't move!" shouted Jamie. "We've got to try to brace the wagon so it doesn't slip any more."

"How long will that take?" she yelled.

"Not long. But you *mustn't* move!"

Fortune set her mind to staying still. It seemed that as soon as Jamie had told her not to move her position became unbearable, as if the very thought of being forced to stay still made her muscles wildly rebellious.

She was surrounded by tools, cans, cookware, and loose clothing. The wound on her head began to throb. The dripping blood forced her to close one eye. Mrs. Watson's hand seemed like an iron claw on her arm.

Fortune heard a jumble of voices outside. The men were arguing, speaking rapidly, their voices colliding so that it was hard to understand them. She heard a new voice and recognized it as that of Abner Simpson. Despite her dislike of the wagon master, she felt better knowing he was there.

"Get a rope here—and another around that wheel," she heard Simpson order. "You men got those? Good. Now let's try to get those women out!"

"Fortune, have you got that rope around Mrs. Watson?" called Jamie.

"Not yet!"

"Well, go ahead and give it a try."

Fortune took a deep breath, then bent forward with the rope.

The wagon crashed to its side.

With a cry of terror she saw the wooden side crack and the cover rip. Their supplies pressed against the opening, tore it wide open, and began to spill into the chasm beyond.

Fortune felt herself sliding toward the opening as well.

CHAPTER THIRTEEN

If Fortune hadn't wrapped the rope Mr. Hyatt had given her around her arm, both she and Mrs. Watson would have been lost to the abyss at once. As it was, they were dangling like links at the end of a chain, and Mrs. Watson's life depended on how long they could manage to cling to each other.

Outside they could hear frantic shouts from the men. Below them was the ghastly drop.

"Close your eyes!" ordered Fortune, tightening her grip on Mrs. Watson's arm.

Mrs. Watson groaned, but did as Fortune told her.

Fortune felt as if her arms were being slowly but surely pulled from their sockets. The rope had tightened around her right wrist, cutting off the circulation. Mrs. Watson's full weight dangled from her other hand.

Suddenly the older woman moaned. "I can't do it, Fortune. I can't hold on any longer."

A surge of fear ripped through Fortune as she felt Mrs. Watson's hand slipping from hers. With the fear came unsuspected strength, and she tightened her own grip as if her hand were made of iron.

"Don't you dare give up," she ordered sharply. "Don't you dare! I promised my father I would get us to California, and I am, by God, going to do it. And I'm taking you with us!"

"I can't," sobbed Mrs. Watson. "I can't do it!"

"You have to!" hissed Fortune. She wanted to scream herself—it felt like she was being ripped in half. But she refused to let go. Closing her eyes, she put herself back in the dingy room where her father had died and whispered over and over, "I promise, Papa. I promise I'll hold the troupe together."

She was still whispering when a sudden movement made her realize that the wagon was being pulled upward.

A thud, a scraping sound, and they were almost level. She heard the men shouting again. The wagon stopped moving, and she realized that the back wheels had caught on the ledge.

Again the wagon began to rock. A series of short, sharp jolts, and suddenly they were over the top.

Fortune cried out in relief and let go of Mrs. Watson. Her arms were throbbing with pain, yet so stiff she could scarcely move them. A burst of voices signaled Jamie and Walter scrambling into the wagon from the back, while Mr. Patchett, Edmund, and Aaron came in from the front. Their questions—"Are you all right? Are you hurt?"—spilled over one another so rapidly that Fortune could hardly think. But somehow she was on her feet, hugging each of them, even Edmund, in turn.

Each of them but Jamie, who was on his knees beside Mrs. Watson, shaking her gently, trying to bring her out of her stupor.

When she finally opened her eyes, she looked around, blinked in bewilderment, then moaned, "Oh, Minerva."

Plunkett's Players stood in a forlorn circle looking at the small pile of supplies on the ground. It was a dismal picture, and no doubt about it. Most of what they owned had disappeared in the crevice where they had nearly lost Fortune and Mrs. Watson as well. Tools, food, the properties and costumes that had survived the fire in Busted Heights—all were now scattered at the bottom of the cliff.

"So much for Jamie's great bargains," said

Aaron sardonically. "What a waste of money that was."

Jamie flushed. Fortune was almost angry with him for not lashing back. To her surprise, she did it for him, snapping, "Well, if you had been driving more carefully, it wouldn't have happened anyway!"

It was Aaron's turn to flush. If anyone had suspected that the accident was mere carelessness on his part, the question had been resolved when the wagon was finally safe and they had peered into the abyss where it had nearly disappeared. At the bottom could be seen the wreckage of two other wagons.

Even so, Aaron had been extremely harsh on himself about the mishap, and Fortune would have given a lot to take back her sharp words.

"Fault is not the issue," said Mr. Patchett, breaking the uncomfortable silence. "The issue is, what are we going to do now?"

"Why not do what you do best?" suggested Jamie.

Fortune looked at him suspiciously. "What do you mean?"

"Put on a show."

"This is hardly the place for theatrics," said Mr. Patchett, glancing around at the circle of wagons.

Fortune followed his gaze. Her proud heart, ill at ease with accepting help from anyone, was troubled by the knowledge that they would never have made it without the help of the others. That help had continued even after the wagon had been pulled back from the brink of disaster, when Frank Hyatt and some other men had temporarily repaired the damages so the troupe could keep up with the wagon train until nightfall. Whatever problems they still faced, she did not want to ask for any more help. Whatever they needed now, they had to earn.

Walter's voice brought her back to the present. "I think the boy's got a point!"

"Minerva, yes!" cried Mrs. Watson, a look of excitement flashing in her eyes. "I was getting rusty anyway!"

"But we lost most of our props and costumes—"

"What difference does that make?" asked Edmund, to the surprise of nearly everyone. "These people won't care. They want entertainment, not perfection."

"That's exactly the point," said Jamie. "They'd love to see a show . . . any show. And we won't charge money. We'll take things in trade: food, clothing, tools—whatever someone can spare."

The group was beginning to get caught up in the idea. Suddenly Fortune felt herself excited by it, too. *I've missed it,* she thought in surprise. *I've actually missed acting!*

They began to prepare for the evening meal—largely a matter of gathering fuel, starting a fire, and letting Jamie cook. During it all they continued chattering about the idea. Excitement was taking hold of them, a sense that maybe a show really was the answer to their problems. Somehow, before the meal was over, it was no longer a question of if they should do it, but of when and how.

Mr. Patchett began to wax nostalgic. "I do miss the shows we used to do."

"You mean back when we were trying to be good?" asked Walter. Fortune was surprised by the bitter tone in the question.

"What was your best show?" asked Jamie quickly.

"*Hamlet,*" said the three older actors, almost in unison.

"Why not do it again?"

"These rubes don't want Shakespeare," said Edmund scornfully.

"I don't know," said Mr. Patchett. He hesitated, as if speaking against his better judgment. "They're doing a lot of Shakespeare out in San Francisco."

"The Booth family has been out there, too," said Mrs. Watson dreamily. "I wonder if we'll ever meet them."

Fortune smiled. Mrs. Watson had been longing

to meet the great Junius Brutus Booth for as long as she could remember. Her smile faded as she heard Walter's next words.

"Don't make any difference," he said mournfully. "We don't have a Hamlet. Not since we lost John."

The moment of painful silence that fell over the group ended when Jamie said softly, "I know the part."

Aaron snorted in derision.

"And I'm the King of Siam," said Edmund.

"Let's hear 'To be, or not to be,' " said Mr. Patchett.

Fortune started to object, but held her tongue.

Slowly, without standing up, without striking a dramatic pose, Jamie began to recite the famous Act Three soliloquy.

> *"To be, or not to be—that is the question.*
> *Whether 'tis nobler in the mind to suffer*
> *The slings and arrows of outrageous fortune,*
> *Or to take arms against a sea of troubles*
> *And, by opposing, end them. . . . "*

His voice was soft at first, as if he were genuinely wondering whether it was better to live or not. His eyes were distant, unfocused, and Fortune had the feeling that for him the fire, the wagons, everyone around them had faded into the distance. When he stood a moment later she caught her breath; the movement had been both unconscious and perfect.

The fire flickered over his face; his voice grew more intense, anguished, as he questioned his being, his worth, the worth of all men. It rang out for a moment, clear and pure, challenging the stars themselves, then sank to an aching whisper on the closing words, "'Be all my sins remember'd.'"

Fortune sat breathless, stunned. Was this the same boy who had rushed onstage and blurted out his lines when they tried to plug him into *The Squire and the Lady*? The bumpkin she had laughed at back in Busted Heights?

"'Do you know me, my lord?'" asked Walter, jumping to a different part in the play.

"'Excellent well; you are a fishmonger.'"

"Excellent indeed!" hooted Walter in delight. "How do you know it so well?"

"My father taught me," said Jamie, shaking his head as if he were being roused from a trance.

"He taught you well," said Mr. Patchett. "Excellent well."

Mrs. Watson said nothing. But she was staring at Jamie in a very strange way.

By the time the players were ready to unveil their version of *Hamlet* a week later, the generosity of their fellow travelers had forced them to change their plans. Instead of a performance for which they took things in trade, it was given free, as a thank-you for all that had been shared with them.

It had been a difficult week. The troupe's version of the play had been drastically trimmed in some spots to make up for the fact that they only had seven actors. As a result, Jamie had had to unlearn many lines and grasp the transitions they had created to get past the scenes that required more actors than they had. Aaron had been alternately helpful and sullen, genuinely taken with what Jamie could do, and at the same time resentful of it.

Jamie himself seemed in a daze at times.

Can he really do it? wondered Fortune nervously. *Knowing the part, even acting it with us, is different from playing it in front of an audience. He's never done a major role before. What if he freezes on us?*

She closed her mind to the possibility. She was nervous enough as it was, since she herself had not played Ophelia in nearly a year.

Worse, her own emotions had threatened to get the best of her several times during the week. Hamlet was her father's favorite role, and his best one. At first she had been swept up by Jamie's power in repeating the lines. But later, as they had worked on it, she found the play bringing back painful memories. She wasn't sure she would make it through the performance herself.

The night before the show Jamie found her sitting beneath a great oak tree. Though she had come there to be alone, somehow his presence did not bother her.

"Mind if I sit down?"

When she shook her head, he folded his legs and settled beside her.

He's gotten more graceful, thought Fortune. *That's Mrs. Watson's doing. She's really helped him a lot.*

"Tired?" Jamie's voice was soft and pleasant, almost like the wind rustling softly through the oak leaves above her.

"Uh-huh. I don't think I could move if I tried."

"Will you be ready for tomorrow night?"

Fortune laughed. "A Plunkett is always ready to go onstage." She sighed and leaned her head back against the tree. "That's our motto."

"You don't sound like you mean it."

Fortune shifted uncomfortably. An owl flew overhead, then settled onto a branch three or four trees away. They heard a sudden patter of rain on the leaves, but just as they were ready to run for the camp, it stopped.

"I don't," said Fortune.

She closed her eyes. Against her will tears began to seep from beneath her lids, trickling down her cheek.

Jamie reached over to brush them away. Fortune stiffened for a moment, then decided to relax and accept the gesture.

"It's funny," he said. "You come from an acting family, and you're tired of acting. I come from a plain-folks family, and I can't get enough of you people. I want to talk about the theater all day long. Do you suppose we always want something different from what we have?"

"I don't know," said Fortune. "That sure would make life complicated."

"It's pretty complicated already," said Jamie, an odd note in his voice. "I wonder if it's even stranger than that. Sometimes I think we're attracted to the people that are most different from us. Look at you . . . you're smart and sophisticated. You've done all that traveling . . ."

"Hush," said Fortune.

Jamie nodded. "I won't say another word," he promised. "As long as you stay here beside me."

Fortune leaned back against the tree. "It's a deal," she whispered.

It was early in July. They had scheduled the show to start at 7:30, to take advantage of the natural light as long as it lasted. Torches had been placed around the playing area, to be lit as necessary. The wagon, stripped of its covering, provided a platform for some of the action. The canvas itself provided a backdrop. Chairs had been borrowed to make thrones for Queen Gertrude and King Claudius.

Everything was in readiness.

Nearly the entire population of the wagon people had gathered to see the performance, bringing with them chairs, stools, and logs to sit on. A restless buzzing filled the air. It was interrupted when Walter pounded on the base of the wagon with a huge stick. (Normally he would have used a drum; unfortunately, it had been lost with the rest of their materials.) He was dressed as the ghost of Hamlet's father; and in the gloom created by the evening shade, his flour-whitened face looked truly eerie.

"Welcome, friends!" he intoned. "Welcome, lovers of the arts! Welcome to *The Tragical History of Hamlet, Prince of Denmark,* as written by one William Shakespeare, and performed by the illustrious Plunkett's Players, late of Charleston and bound for California!"

The words earned a burst of applause.

"Oh, they're ripe," said Mrs. Watson gleefully. Standing next to her, behind a blanket they had strung between two poles, Fortune was uncharacteristically nervous. With a jolt she realized the cause: these were people they had lived with for over two months and would continue to live with for some time. Unlike the normal audience— never seen again, faceless, unknown—these were friends, acquaintances, partners on the road to adventure.

I care what they think! she told herself uncomfortably. *I can't remember the last time I felt this way.*

Suddenly Jamie was standing beside her. He put his hands on her shoulders, turned her toward him, and kissed her on the cheek.

"Be wonderful," he whispered.

To her amazement, she was. Not immediately. But from the moment she traded her first lines with Jamie, there was a fire between them that she had never experienced on the stage before. He was unbelievably good himself, his eyes tragic and haunted, his voice filled with pain and power.

It brought out the best in her. Always before, when her father had acted the role, no matter how good he was, he was still her father.

But Jamie was not Jamie. He *was* Hamlet. And in becoming that melancholy Dane, he transformed Fortune Plunkett, too. For the first time in more than a hundred performances, she became

Ophelia, loved as Ophelia, ached as Ophelia, wept as Ophelia. It was wonderful. It was agony. She felt as if her heart was being torn in half.

"Do you know what you're doing out there?" hissed Mrs. Watson, grabbing her arm between scenes. "Do you have any idea what you are doing to that audience?"

Fortune shook her head numbly.

Mrs. Watson stared at her. "Good," she said at last. "Maybe it's better that way."

And when Aaron, as Laertes, and Jamie, as Hamlet fought their final duel, she found herself behind the blanket sobbing as if her heart would break.

In her heart she knew that something had happened. She had been touched by the spirit of her father, and acting would never be the same for her again.

CHAPTER FOURTEEN

Spurred on by their success, the troupe performed several more times during the journey; another *Hamlet,* done at the insistence of those who had missed it the first time and been told by the others in the wagon train how good it was; a remarkable *Othello,* with Walter and Mr. Patchett glowing in the roles of Othello and Iago; and of course their old standby, *The Widow's Daughter.*

A few of these performances were for their fellow travelers. The majority of them were for people in the isolated forts and tiny settlements along the way. Once they performed for a single family in return for the best hot meal they had had in three months.

They took a curious pleasure in these performances. Their audiences were hungry to be entertained, and in response the troupe performed as it rarely had before.

"It's not just a hunger for entertainment," said Mr. Patchett, when Fortune mentioned this one night. "They're hungry for something for their souls. Get a roof over a man's head, get him fed regular, and there's another need that starts to grow, a need to think and feel that can gnaw you just as sure as hunger gnaws your belly when you've been too long without a meal."

Even so, it struck Fortune more than once how ironic it was that the finest shows Plunkett's Players had ever done should be not on the fancy stages of the East, but on the bare ground and makeshift platforms of a crude, unsettled land.

Papa, I wish you were with us, she thought over and over as the troupe continued to jounce and rattle their way westward. *I wish you could meet Jamie. He reminds me of you so much, the way you must have been when you were young. I think you'd like him.*

Crossing the mountains was the hardest thing any of them had ever done; and by the time the trip was nearing completion, they were worn to the point of exhaustion. They had pushed the wagon up steep slopes, even Mrs. Watson joining the effort. Sometimes going down the other side of a slope was even harder, and it took all the strength the troupe had to keep the wagon from barreling forward and running over the horses, even with its brakes set at their highest level.

In one way their accident proved a blessing in disguise. While they had already been traveling with a lighter load than most of the pilgrims, the accident had left their wagon almost empty—which spared them the slow, painful peeling away of belongings that they watched the other families make as the trail grew tougher and their animals were worn to the point of exhaustion, or even death. The road to California was littered with castoff things that families had hoped to take across and been forced to abandon once they were nearly there. Fortune spent half a day walking with Becky Hyatt because the girl was so distraught over her father's decision to cast off a beautiful wooden dresser that had belonged to her grandmother.

"It was all we had of Nana," Becky sobbed over and over, leaning against Fortune.

She didn't question that her father had made the right decision; two of their oxen had died already, and the rest of the team simply could not bear the load. But it had cut the girl to the heart.

Despite the despair and exhaustion, the troupe also experienced a growing sense of anticipation. Every night they sat spinning out hopes and dreams about the shows they would put on in California, the theater they would build.

Sometimes they would act out favorite scenes as they sat around their fire, Aaron and Jamie competing to give the best performance. Often other travelers would gather round, listening intently, not saying a word. Usually when this happened, Fortune would get out her guitar, Walter his fiddle, and they would begin to play and sing as they had that night in Independence.

Five or six times there were impromptu dances, the weary men and women seeming to shed their exhaustion as they whirled each other about in the firelight.

When Fortune wished to bring such evenings to a close, she would nod to Walter and he would put away his fiddle. Then she would play alone, singing a quiet song she had written herself, about being a stranger alone in a strange new world.

> *"When I rise up*
> *And look around,*
> *My home I cannot see,*
> *For I have wandered*
> *Far away . . .*
> *What will become of me?"*

When she finished, the weary travelers would nod and sigh, and slip quietly into the night.

Yet Fortune knew that many of them were not

really far from home. They had their families, and home was in the ties that held them together. Though she liked that idea, it also gave her a strange sense of melancholy, stirring in her a sense of incompleteness she couldn't quite explain, nor even willingly admit to.

During this time Jamie and Aaron continued a strange, unspoken courtship of her, each paying her much attention, neither saying aloud what they were feeling.

To her surprise, it was Edmund who finally mentioned it.

"You ought to stop this game, you know," he said one evening, coming up beside her unexpectedly as she gathered wood for the cooking fire.

"What do you mean?"

"Oh, don't play games with me, too," he said curtly. "My personality may not thrill you, but you know I'm not stupid. You'd better make a choice, or you'll lose them both."

When she remained stubbornly silent, he laughed and said, "The funny thing is, you've already made your choice. And everyone knows it except the three of you."

"Go away, Edmund."

"I will, when I'm finished. I know you don't like me. I don't even know why I'm bothering to tell you this, except that I liked *you* once, for a little while. That, and I hate seeing people act stupid."

"You have a wonderful way with words," she said, savagely tearing a dead branch from a tree.

"I know. Wins me friends everywhere I go. Look, Fortune—if you're not careful . . . Oh, forget it. I don't know why I bothered."

He turned and stalked away, his back rigid, a cloud of ice in the air behind him.

"Wait. What did you mean everyone knows? Edmund? *Edmund!*"

It was too late; he would never tell her now.

Is it that obvious? How can it be, when I don't know myself? She stamped her foot, feeling suddenly stubborn. Who said she wanted either one of them?

Still fuming, she carried the armload of wood back to the wagon.

"Jamie was looking for you," said Mrs. Watson when she saw her.

Fortune didn't answer.

"So was Aaron," continued the older woman, smiling slyly. "Don't think I ever saw two cats so intent on the same mouse."

"Don't *you* start," said Fortune sullenly.

"What did I say?"

"Nothing! Forget it!" She threw down the wood and stomped away from the wagon.

*   *   *

"We've got to make a decision," Mr. Patchett said to her that night.

Fortune sighed. Sometimes it seemed that all she did was make decisions.

"What is it?" she asked.

"Whether to go straight to San Francisco or spend some time touring the mining camps before we go."

"Why would we do that?" asked Mrs. Watson indignantly. "I can't wait to get to San Francisco!"

"Alas, we won't be able to do much when we get there," said Mr. Patchett. "We're flat broke. And it's not as though we've got a booking waiting for us when we get there. I think we might be better off touring the camps for a while. That way we may be able to build up a stake, not to mention a reputation."

Fortune let the others talk for a while. She had learned that if she listened carefully to what they had to say—and made sure they *knew* she was listening—that when she made her decision she would have fewer complaints from those who were not happy with it.

In this case it was only Mrs. Watson who thought they should go straight to San Francisco. "I can't live like this anymore," she moaned. "I need some civilization."

"Civilization requires money," said Fortune.

Which was how the matter was decided.

Two days later—following directions provided by Abner Simpson (who seemed both amazed that they had made it this far and somewhat disappointed that they were leaving)—they separated from the wagon train and headed for a mining town.

Becky Hyatt walked a half a mile or so with them, and for a little while Fortune thought she was going to ask to come along. In the end she hugged them all, then threw her arms around Aaron, kissed him on the lips, burst into tears, and ran back toward her family's wagon.

Aaron stood looking after her in astonishment, until Mr. Patchett clapped him on the shoulder and asked him to get the wagon moving again.

They had made it to California. It was time to start digging for gold, the Plunkett's Players way.

CHAPTER FIFTEEN

Nothing, not all they had read, all they had heard, all they had imagined, prepared them for what they found when they rolled into Mad Jack's Gulch. The town was a rowdy, roaring collection of bustling saloons, seedy hotels, makeshift cabins, and a lonely, whitewashed church. The streets were filled with the wildest collection of folk they had ever seen—the fabled forty-niners, dressed in everything from flannel and blue jeans to silk and top hats. Music tinkled from behind the barroom doors. A beautiful woman leaned down from a second-story window in one of the hotels, calling out to the men in language that made Fortune blush.

And rooms were ten dollars a night.

"Ten dollars!" exploded Fortune. "What is this, a hotel or a palace?"

"This is gold country," replied the clerk. "Take it or leave it."

She went into a hurried conference with Mr. Patchett. After a series of negotiations, some of them carried out at the top of her lungs, she managed to rent two rooms for twenty dollars, a victory for the clerk—with the addition of extra mattresses for the men's room at no extra charge, a victory for Fortune.

About that time Walter came into the lobby, his face ashen.

"What's the matter?" asked Fortune.

"I found a building."

"Then what's the problem?" she persisted, feeling like a prompter.

"The owner wants a hundred dollars for one night."

"He wants *what?*"

"A hundred dollars," repeated Walter glumly.

"Come on," said Fortune, grabbing him by the arm. "The rest of you get our things into the rooms. I'll be back in an hour."

The owner of the building was a tall Irishman named Jack Burns. "Look, lady," he said, when Fortune complained about his price, "it ain't worth it to me to let you use the building for less than that. You'll probably burn it down anyway, using candles or lanterns or something so people can see your show."

"We will not!" said Fortune, blushing at the memory of the fire in Busted Heights. "Now look. I can't possibly pay you a hundred dollars to use your building for one night. You can let it sit empty, and make nothing, or you can give me a reasonable price and we'll both be happy."

Forty-five minutes later she and Walter headed back toward the hotel, having hammered out a deal where they would pay Burns fifty dollars in advance and another hundred after the show—a deal that had somehow seemed less painful after Burns told Fortune they could charge ten dollars a seat for the first four rows and still fill them.

"We eat what we came with till after tomorrow night," she told the group when they had assembled in the room she was sharing with Mrs. Watson. Once the groans had died down, she added, "Then we'll know whether coming west was the best thing we ever did—or the craziest."

She didn't add that at the moment she herself had decided it was the craziest.

By the next night Fortune was beginning to think maybe they weren't so crazy after all. Walter had spent the day putting up signs to advertise the show. Edmund and Mr. Patchett had stationed themselves in the hotel lobby, selling advance tickets. And—at the advice of Jack Burns—she, Jamie, Aaron, and

Mrs. Watson had spent some time practicing their scenes on the front porch of the hotel. As Burns had predicted, this attracted a crowd that then dispersed to spread the word a show was in town.

"I don't know how well you're going to do," the clerk had said gloomily that morning. "We had a troupe through here just two weeks ago. Had one of what they call them 'Fairy Stars' with 'em—little girl, maybe eight, nine years old. She sang, acted . . . everything. Even did scenes from *Hamlet,* all dressed up like a prince!"

"Wait till they see *our Hamlet,*" said Fortune confidently.

"I saw that Lola Montez a few months ago," continued the clerk, ignoring Fortune's comment and apparently feeling she should be made aware of his broad experience with the stage. "Down in San Francisco. She did that Spider Dance of hers. Funniest thing I ever saw. She didn't take it too kindly when folks laughed at her, though." He shook his head. "Gotta have a sense of humor if you want to stay alive out here."

The clerk's words had stuck in Fortune's mind, and she recalled them that evening as she looked out at an audience composed of rough-and-ready mining men, elegant dandies, and a scattering of women who ranged from a severely dressed minister's wife to a gaudy creature Mrs. Watson referred to as a "painted strumpet."

"My, doesn't *he* look ripsniptious," said Mrs. Watson, pointing out an elegant-looking man seated in the center of the audience.

"What did you say?" asked Fortune.

"That's mining talk, gosling," said Mrs. Watson, as if she had been in California since the first month of the Gold Rush. "Means he's all spruced up and looking fine."

"I'll remember that."

Then Walter stepped onstage to introduce the show.

Things went well until the third act, when someone in the audience started making whispered comments to his neighbor about the performance. His neighbor's laughter emboldened him, and soon the comments got louder, until there was a circle of laughter in the center of the audience that made it hard for others to hear.

"Quiet!" bellowed someone in front. "I want to hear the show!"

Things did quiet down for a few minutes. Then the self-appointed wit decided to make fun of Edmund's costume, a shabby thing he had patched together to replace one lost in their mountainside accident.

Edmund's eyes grew dark and angry. Fortune, anticipating trouble, began to rush her lines, hoping they could get through the act, which was nearly over, and let things calm down.

No such luck. One more comment from the audience was all it took to push Edmund over the edge. Seething with indignation, he jumped from the stage and barged through the audience until he reached the heckler. Then he drew back and landed a powerful haymaker on his jaw.

After that it was pure pandemonium. Half the audience was on the side of the actors, having been enjoying the play. The other half was all for the locals, no matter what they had done. And both halves, Fortune suspected, enjoyed a good brawl at least as much as a well-done play anyway.

Walter waded into the fray, roaring and swinging his massive arms like an enraged bear. Mrs. Watson hung back until she spotted someone struggling with Mr. Patchett, at which point she picked up a chair and hit the man over the head.

The low point of the whole fiasco came when Fortune decided to join the battle, too. Ducking under the flying fists, most of which were well over her head anyway, she pushed her way toward the oaf who had started the whole problem. Spotting him, she wound up and let fly with a solid punch, which landed squarely in Jamie Halleck's eye.

*   *   *

"I was on my way to rescue you from the mob," he told her the next morning as he poked ruefully at the spectacular shiner that decorated the right side of his face. "I should have let the mob rescue me from you instead!" He winced and added, "I think I would have preferred another fire."

"That would have cost more," replied Fortune glumly. "As it was all we had to do was pay for the broken chairs."

"I suppose you've got a point," said Jamie. "Is there anything left?"

"A hundred dollars."

"Well, that's more than we started out with."

"Breakfast cost thirty."

"Ouch!"

"Are you referring to the price tag, or your eye?"

"Both."

They walked in silence for a while. It was a beautiful morning, golden and sundrenched, with just enough of a late September chill to make the air almost painfully sweet. They had left the hotel separately after breakfast and run into each other at the edge of town. By mutual consent they had walked together up the bank of the river, eager to be away from outsiders.

"Mrs. Watson says it was the biggest conbob-beration she ever saw," said Fortune after a while.

"Beg pardon?"

"That's miner talk," said Fortune, imitating Mrs. Watson perfectly. "It means a brawl."

"Well, I'll agree with her on that. What got into Edmund, anyway?"

"Theatrical temperament. He can't stand being laughed at." Fortune recalled the desk clerk's prophetic words about needing a sense of humor in mining country. As if reading her mind, Jamie started to laugh himself.

"And just what is so funny?" she demanded.

"Oh, I was just remembering Mrs. Watson knocking over that miner," he said, still chuckling. "She packs quite a wallop." He poked at his eye again. "So do you, for that matter."

"I'm sorry," she said, not for the first time.

"No, no. It's good to know you can defend yourself. I never did like weak women." He smiled at her. "It's getting warm," he said, changing the subject. "Let's go wading!"

Fortune hesitated. Back East her mother would have been scandalized at the prospect. But here in California the rules seemed different. She looked longingly at the small stream that bubbled along beside them. Her feet *were* feeling hot and tired.

"Good idea," she said suddenly. And at once, as though by the very act of shedding her inhibition, the whole world seemed richer and sweeter. She became more aware of the increased warmth of the sun as it had risen in the sky, of the calling birds about them, the smell of the forest, and most of all the presence of someone very special beside her.

How can he not be angry with me? she wondered, suddenly feeling very safe with him. For a moment, almost against her will, she remembered the feel of his arms about her when he had carried her out of the fire months ago.

"This is a good spot," said Jamie. He took her arm and helped her sit on the thick moss.

He has nice feet, she thought, watching from the corner of her eye as he slipped off his shoes and socks and rolled up his trouser legs. She slipped off her own boots and looked at her feet appraisingly. *These aren't bad, either,* she thought with satisfaction.

"Come on," said Jamie, jumping up. "Let's go!"

Laughing, they splashed into the water. It was cold, but the air was warm. Great trees arched over them, filtering the sunlight so that it fell in pools and puddles of gold about them.

"Beautiful, isn't it?" said Jamie, gesturing to the forest that surrounded them.

186

"Uh-huh. Almost scary. It's so big."

"I don't think anything can seem big after those mountains we crossed."

Fortune thought of the mountains, and how Jamie had kept the group going at the worst stage of the crossing with his irrepressible good humor. She felt a surge of closeness to him and moved imperceptibly nearer.

Without a word he led her to the far side of the stream. They sat on a rock outcropping, warmed by a patch of sunlight.

Jamie was stiff, almost rigid, as he sat staring into the water.

Say it! Fortune thought. *Tell me what you're thinking!*

"Fortune, I . . ." He stopped, then tried again. "Fortune . . ."

Just then they spotted it, a dull yellow glow in the water between their feet. Without a word they reached for it, their fingers entering the water simultaneously. Then, as if drawn by a magnet, their hands moved from what they had been reaching for and instead closed over each other.

Still not speaking, Jamie stood and drew Fortune to her feet.

She looked up into his eyes. *I think I'm going to die. I didn't know my heart could beat so fast . . . or that his arms could feel so good. What's happening to me?*

And then there was no time to think of what was happening as he drew her closer. His arms tightened about her and his hands slid over her dress and his lips pressed against hers.

There were no questions now, no answers, no right, no wrong, no night, no day—only the two of them standing in the ancient forest, clinging desperately to each other, admitting what both of them had known from the very first instant they saw each other . . . that there was no one else in the world for either one of them.

"I love you," he whispered, his voice soft and husky. "I've loved you from the first moment I saw you, loved you without stopping ever since, loved you while you tried to make up your mind, loved you while you were laughing at me, wondering about me, angry at me, hating me, teasing me . . ."

And then he couldn't speak anymore, because her lips had covered his, and words were no longer necessary.

CHAPTER SIXTEEN

Fortune sighed contentedly. "Probably you should have just grabbed me and run away with me that first day in Busted Heights," she said, leaning against him.

"I doubt it would have done much good. You're the type who wants a man to prove himself."

"I suppose I am," she said, snuggling closer. "Of course, you did that some time ago."

"Yes, but you wouldn't admit it!"

She laughed. They were sitting on the bank of the little stream, still dangling their feet in the water. A small bird was flitting back and forth above them, its yellow wings flashing in the sunlight.

I want time to stop. Right here. Right now. There'll never be a moment as perfect as this again anyway.

"It's funny," said Jamie, picking up one of the nuggets resting in her lap. "A lot of people came west to find gold and ended up doing something else. We came west to do something else, and stumbled over a jackpot."

"It's pretty enough," said Fortune, taking the nugget from him and holding it in a sun ray. "But it's hard to imagine people killing each other over it."

"'There is thy gold,'" murmured Jamie, "'worse poison to men's souls, doing more murders in this loathsome world—'"

"Ugh." Fortune shivered. "What's that from?"

"Romeo and Juliet." He lifted her hand, stroking it gently, and dropped another nugget into her palm. "Here's a line I like better: 'This hand was made to handle nought but gold.' That's from one of the Henry plays. But Old Will might have been writing about you."

Fortune closed her fingers over the nugget. She knew which piece it was—the peculiar heart-shaped one they had picked up first, the one that had drawn their hands together, knocking down the wall of reserve that had stood between them, kept them apart.

Jamie pried her fingers open, his hand firm but gentle. "The rest of the gold is for the dream," he said. "Oh, Fortune, we'll go to San Francisco and do such plays! But this nugget will be our keepsake, because it brought us together. I want you to guard it until the time is right. When it is, I'll have it made into a ring . . ."

He closed her hand again, holding it in his, and kissed her softly on the neck.

Walter was clapping his hands with glee. "Gold!" he sang. "Gold, gold, gold, gold, gold. We're rich! I can't believe it. Henry, we're rich!"

He grabbed Mr. Patchett and tried to dance with him.

"Calm down, Walter," said Mr. Patchett patiently. He was trying to be calm himself, but his hands were trembling. "*We're* not rich. Jamie and Fortune are. They found it."

"No," said Jamie firmly. "The gold is for the troupe. We'll go to San Francisco and use it to build the kind of theater you've always dreamed of—do the kind of shows you've dreamed of."

Mr. Patchett placed a hand on Jamie's shoulder. "That's most generous of you, Jamie. But we can't—"

"Oh, don't be a goose, Henry," said Mrs. Watson. "Of course we can. He's one of us, isn't he? Any one of us that found the gold would do the same thing, right?"

She looked around the room. "Right?" she asked again. Suddenly it seemed to dawn on her that more than one person in the room might not

191

be so generous with such a find, and she fell silent.

"Half the gold is Fortune's anyway," said Jamie.

"Well, that settles it," said Edmund. "San Francisco, watch out!" Fortune studied his voice for the usual note of sarcasm. To her surprise, it wasn't there.

Only Aaron had been silent through the jubilation that greeted their announcement and the debate that followed. Looking at him, Fortune wondered if he had realized what had happened between her and Jamie, the way their feelings had been unleashed. Could he read it in their eyes, their faces, the way they glanced at each other?

"The thing is, we've got to keep this quiet," said Jamie. "Maybe there's more gold up there, maybe not. But if we let anyone know what we found, the place will be swarming with men by morning."

"The boy is right," said Mr. Patchett, suddenly serious. "We'd better keep this to ourselves."

"I agree," said Edmund.

Immediately Fortune felt a surge of anxiety, certain that Edmund was planning to go clean the place out himself before anyone else could get there.

She shook her head. Jamie had warned her that the very discovery of gold could cause divisions within the group. She could feel it starting in her own heart.

She ordered herself not to be so suspicious.

Yet she could not shake the nagging sense of discomfort that plagued her as she watched the men go off to celebrate.

As she brooded through the painful weeks that followed, Fortune realized that no matter how strong her premonitions had been, she could never have guessed how quickly disaster would strike—nor from what an unexpected quarter.

It was announced by a frantic midnight knocking on her door, a thundering sound that pulled her from a delicious dream.

"Fortune! Fortune, wake up!"

She clawed her way to wakefulness. Mrs. Watson, as usual, was snoring ferociously beside her.

"Fortune!"

Slightly dazed, Fortune recognized the voice as Aaron's. She felt a chill. Had he come to confront her about Jamie?

More pounding. "Fortune. *Fortune!*"

"All right, all right," she called. "I'm coming!"

As she threw her robe over her nightclothes she was struck by an uncomfortable memory of the last midnight knocking at the door. Surely they weren't going to be run out of town again? That brawl last night was nothing more than a . . . a conbobberation. The miners had them all the time.

Taking a breath to steel herself against whatever problem she was about to face, she opened the door. The palpable fear on Aaron's face sent a wave of hot panic racing down Fortune's spine. The last vestiges of sleep fell away from her like icicles crashing from eaves on a sunny day. "What is it?" she asked. "What's going on?"

"It's Walter. He's in big trouble."

"What kind of trouble?"

Aaron looked on the verge of tears. "We went to the Golden Slipper tonight, to . . . to kind of celebrate the good news."

The cold feeling increased. She remembered the last night her father had gone out drinking.

"Was Jamie with you?"

Aaron looked angry. "No. Listen to me! Walter got separated from the rest of us. After an hour or so Mr. Patchett told me to go find him. He was at one of the gambling tables. Fortune, he . . . he got in over his head. He lost a lot. More than he ever had in his life, probably. If we don't pay it for him, they're apt to . . . to . . ."

He lapsed into a stunned silence.

Her voice was cold. "Will they kill him?"

"Yes."

"How much is it?"

"Everything. All you and Jamie found today. Maybe more."

She felt herself stagger. "How could you let him?" she whispered.

Aaron began to protest.

"Oh, never mind," she snapped. "Be quiet. I've got to think."

But there was nothing to think about. She knew what she had to do. Yet she couldn't bring herself to it right away. "How do you know how much we found today, anyway?" she asked to stall for time.

"Jamie weighed it and told Mr. Patchett. Mr. Patchett told the rest of us."

"You'd make a fine bunch of old women," said Fortune tartly. "Your tongues flapping like . . . Oh, never mind. Wait here."

She went to the trunk the Hyatts had given her after the accident in the mountains. Lifting the lid, she drew out an old sock bulging with the morning's bounty. *Sorry, Papa. I guess this is the end of the dream. But I know you'd do the same thing. You wouldn't let anyone hurt Walter. Or any of the troupe. Not even Edmund. Mama always said you were too softhearted for your own good.* A solitary tear trickled down her cheek. *I guess I'm not that different.*

She carried the gold to Aaron. "Here. Take it. Save his worthless old hide. . . ." She turned away. "Hurry up. Go!"

Before Aaron could move more than a step

from the door, Fortune turned back and asked, "Will it be enough?"

"I don't know. He lost an awful lot. The other men are furious."

A coldness crept over her, seemed to reach all the way to her heart. "Wait a minute."

She was angry at herself for what she was about to do, even though she knew she had no choice.

"Fortune, I've got to get back there. They may not wait as it is. . . ."

"I said wait a minute!" she snapped. Then, almost to herself, she whispered, "We can't take any chances."

Crossing to the bed where Mrs. Watson lay disturbing the night with her snores, Fortune thrust her hand under her own pillow and closed her fingers over the heart-shaped nugget that was to have become her wedding ring.

Forgive me, Jamie, because I may not ever be able to forgive myself. But I can't take a chance with Walter's life . . . not if this would make the difference.

Trembling, she returned to Aaron. "Take this!" she said ferociously. She pressed the nugget into his hand. "Take it, and get out of my sight!"

She waited until he had closed the door, then ran to the bed and threw herself across it, weeping silent, bitter tears. All their dreams, their hopes, their plans for the theater were gone again.

Had Fortune stayed at her door just a moment longer, she might have seen a slightly groggy Jamie Halleck—roused by the disturbance in the hall—open the door of the room he shared with the other men. Just a moment longer, and she might have caught the stricken look on Jamie's face as he watched Aaron Masters softly step away from her room.

She might have seen all that.

If she had, she might have prevented what happened next.

It was Mrs. Watson who found the letter. He had written it in pencil, on blank pages torn from the front of one of his books of Shakespeare, and must have slid the letter under their door sometime during the night.

She handed it to Fortune, who opened it eagerly, but found her excitement turning to horror as she read.

My Dearest Fortune,

I address you that way, even though I now understand that you do not feel the same way toward me. I suppose it marks me as a fool. Even so, it is how I will always think of you—as the dearest person in all the world. I thought the games were over. I thought you were done playing with me, and ready to accept my love.

But when I saw Aaron leave your room tonight I realized that Macbeth was right; life *is* nothing but "a tale told by an idiot, full of sound and fury, and signifying nothing."

At least, that is the case with my life.

I cannot tell you how that sight burns within me. I thought my heart would burst with pain when I watched Aaron leave your room. Fortune! Didn't this morning mean anything to you? Was all that passed between us a charade, words without meaning, kisses without love?

I cannot stay with the troupe any longer. I do not know if you love Aaron. If so, I wish you all the happiness in the world with him. If not, then I hope you do find love someday. Because you deserve to be loved. And when you find that love, I hope it is even half as deep and half as true as the love I bear for you. Because then I know he will never be able to hurt you, and will do all that he can to make you happy.

I can't bear to see your face again, so I have to go now. To be with you and know you are not mine, to see you and not kiss you, be near you and not embrace you, love you and know it is all in vain . . .

I have to leave. If I had any sense, I would try to forget you.

I have no sense. As long as I live, I will hold you in my heart and cherish the memory of this morning. False as those moments were, they were the dearest I shall ever know.

Please make my excuses to the others. I hate to leave you at this time, but I am sure you understand.

May God be with you.

Your adoring servant,
Jamie Halleck

CHAPTER SEVENTEEN

Her cry was like that of a wounded animal. "Noooo!" she shrieked. "No! Oh, damn them, damn them. What have they done to us. What have they done to *him*? Oh, Jamie!"

Her initial hysteria turned rapidly to a deadly calm. "Find him," she said coldly. "Now!"

Mrs. Watson scuttled from the room and roused the others. Without telling them exactly what had happened, she told them that Jamie was missing, and they needed to find him. The worried actors spread out and searched the town, the little valley along the stream, even the forest.

As for Fortune, she made her way back to the stream where she and Jamie had found the nugget, praying that she might find him, tell him what had happened.

But he had vanished. To find him was impossible, for despite the rapid growth of the last four years, the area was still a great wilderness, easily capable of swallowing a man—especially one who *wanted* to disappear.

Late that evening, when they had all returned to the hotel, Aaron took her aside.

"I managed to save this out last night," he said, handing her the heart-shaped nugget. She bit her lip, but said nothing. She was beyond bitterness, beyond thanks.

He reached down, placed his hand against her cheek, his touch gentle, tender.

"Look, I know how things are with you and Jamie," he said. He spoke slowly, the words clearly difficult for him. "I've known for a long time, actually. Probably before you did."

She started to speak, but he cut her off. "No, it's all right. Because I also know that I'm not what you need." He turned away, and when he spoke, his voice was soft. "I don't think I'll ever . . ." He let the words hang, the thought unfinished. "It's not you, Fortune. It's me. Don't worry about it."

She reached out, touched his arm.

When he turned back to her, saw the tears streaming down her face, he reached out and gathered her into his arms.

"Go ahead," he whispered. "Cry it out. I made

a lousy boyfriend. Maybe I can do better as a big brother."

It seemed as if Jamie had taken the heart of the troupe with him. Walter, stricken with remorse, seemed to age twenty years in a day, somehow shrinking into himself. He walked about wearing a mask of tragedy that almost equaled the sorrow Fortune felt inside. Mr. Patchett was silent, the silence of a great emptiness. Mrs. Watson, on the other hand, raged on at length about fools and drunks and gamblers, making everyone feel generally worse than they already did. Even Aaron and Edmund seemed to be mourning his disappearance.

Fortune read the letter over and over again.

On Friday it began to rain, a slow, steady drizzle that seemed somehow appropriate.

Throwing on her cloak, Fortune went out to walk under the weeping sky.

The streets were deserted. Fortune clutched Jamie's letter in her hand, holding it carefully beneath her cloak to protect it from the rain. She wandered aimlessly along the muddy byways. Music tinkled from the saloons, mingling with laughter, shouts of anger, even an occasional gunshot.

Yet she felt as if she were a million miles from

anyone, more alone and lost than she had ever dreamed possible.

What do I do now? How do you go on when you finally figure out what you want, and have it snatched away before . . . before . . .

She began to sob. *Jamie, you should have waited. You should have trusted me!*

She stopped, leaned her head against a rough wooden wall. The rain beat against her insistently, whispering, "Fool, fool. What was to trust? The flirt who played one man against the other while she made up her mind? How could he trust you when you toyed with him and Aaron for a hundred days, a thousand miles."

She moaned and pushed her fists against the wall. *But I did do it. I made up my mind. Oh, Jamie, heart of my heart, I made up my mind!*

With a low moan she started to slide toward the ground.

"There you are!" said an unfamiliar voice. "I've been looking for you!"

Fortune found herself looking into the most remarkable pair of eyes she had ever seen. Broad, dark and deep set, they peered out at her from the depths of a thick riding cloak that had been pulled up to protect its wearer from the slashing rain.

"Who are you?" she asked warily.

The stranger chose to ignore the question.

Extending a slender white hand, she said, "Get up, child. This behavior is not suited to one of your stature." Her voice was marked with a mild accent that Fortune found hard to place.

"Who are you?" repeated Fortune, taking the woman's hand. Then, "What do you mean? What stature do I have?"

"You are an actress. Not merely an actress, but a Plunkett, the last of one of the great acting families of our time."

Fortune felt her head begin to reel. What was going on here? She stared at the stranger through the rain. She appeared to be quite beautiful, though it was hard to tell for certain. "Who are you?" she asked a third time, trying to keep her voice from shaking.

"My name is Lola Montez," said the woman. "Though I am sometimes known as the Countess of Landsfeld, or," and this last was said with a hint of wicked amusement, "the Witch of Bavaria."

Fortune barely restrained herself from making a curtsy. "What do you want with me?" she whispered.

Lola smiled. "I've come to take you home," she said, tightening her grip on Fortune's hand.

When they returned to the hotel, Lola insisted on sneaking in to avoid attracting attention. They went to the second floor. Fortune didn't have to call the others together; they were already clustered in one room—to talk about her, she suspected. Leading Lola into the room, she said, "Mrs. Watson, gentlemen of the troupe, I give you . . . Lola Montez!"

She could see the skepticism on Mr. Patchett's face. But Mrs. Watson had studied Lola's exploits long enough and carefully enough to recognize her on sight. She immediately dropped to a curtsy.

Lola laughed and pulled her to her feet.

"But what has brought you to us?" asked Mrs. Watson, when she had recovered herself. She had taken a seat on the bed and was fanning herself in astonishment.

"Fortune's father asked me to look out for you."

The unexpected statement caused Fortune's knees to buckle. "What do you mean?"

Lola smiled at her tenderly. "Your dear Papa, when he was dying, wrote letters to many of his friends, asking us to keep an eye out for you, to help you if we could."

"You were a friend of my father's?" asked Fortune in astonishment.

"I met him many years ago in Europe, when he was touring with a company of Shakespearians. He was a fine player your father, one of the great Hamlets of our time."

Fortune felt her heart twist a little when Lola

said that. It reminded her not only of her father, but of the stunning night when she and Jamie had first performed the play.

"Papa never even told me he knew you," she whispered.

Lola's face darkened. "Men often do not speak of me to their families. I am too much the scandal, you know? But your father wrote me, and to other friends as well, to ask us to watch out for you. Those of us who live upon the stage must stick together, you see? Our community is small, and we must help each other. So I have been waiting for word of you. So have many others. But you came to where I am; you came to California!" She smiled. "It did not take long for news of your last battle—excuse me, your last *performance*—to reach me. Juicy news travels fast. My people got it to me quickly. So I came to look for you."

"Your people?"

Lola laughed. "I have eyes everywhere. Sooner or later everyone in California who is in the theater comes to Grass Valley to see Lola. And then they tell me what is happening. It is a funny place, Grass Valley. They do not know what to think of me yet. But they know I have made it special. Before I came, all they had was gold. Now? Now they have Lola!"

Her proclamation made it seem like a great victory for Grass Valley.

"Now, Fortune, you must tell me, for I am dying of curiosity—did you accomplish your mission in that strange little town, Flat Busted?"

"You mean Busted Heights?" asked Fortune eagerly. "Do you know what my father wanted us to do there?"

"It appears that you have already done it," said Lola, gazing at Aaron and Edmund. "Which of you was it?"

"Which of who was what?" asked Aaron, expressing everyone's confusion.

"Which of you is the son of Julian Beck?"

Mrs. Watson cried out in horror, then fell to the floor in a dead faint.

When they had propped her up in bed and shooed the men out of the room, Mrs. Watson told Fortune and Lola her story.

"Julian Beck was my first husband. I married him when I was sixteen. He was nine years older than me." She sighed. "Twenty-five seemed very old and wise to me back then."

"I have known many men," said Lola. "Few of them were wise, no matter what their age."

Mrs. Watson continued, telling her story directly to Fortune. "Julian and I had to marry in secret, because my father did not approve of the match." She reached out and took Fortune's hand. "You don't know how lucky you were, child, to have a father such as yours. He would have understood, whether he approved or not. My father did not understand. When he found out our secret while Julian was on tour, he sent me into hiding."

"To keep you away from Julian?"

"Partly. But mostly because I was going to have Julian's baby."

"Men!" said Lola. She spit on the floor, then lit herself a cigarette, which caused Fortune to blink in astonishment. She had never seen a woman smoke before.

Mrs. Watson's tears were flowing freely now, streaming down her cheeks. "When my baby was born, they took him away from me. They told me he was dead."

"They lied," said Lola. She moved to sit next to Mrs. Watson. "It was not that way at all. Julian's best friend—your father, Fortune—found out the rest of the story much later. Here is what happened: When Julian discovered where the child had been taken he stole it—" She laughed bitterly. "Stole his own son, what a crime! Then Julian changed his name and fled west, all the way to Missouri, which at that time was like going to the uttermost ends of the earth."

Mrs. Watson was trembling. "When I could, I fled, too—fled my home and became an actress. I did it partly to spite my father. I did it partly because I was already such a fallen woman that it made no difference to me what people thought of me. But I did it mostly so that I could be near Julian's friends, John and Laura Plunkett." She reached out to Lola, took her hand. "But I never knew my baby had lived. Why didn't John tell me?"

"At first he didn't know," said Lola. "He spent years trying to find out what had happened to his best friend. He told me as much of the story as he knew when I met him in Europe. At that time he had learned the first part of the story—and learned as well that Julian was dead. But he did not yet know whether the child still lived. Nor did he know what it would mean to the boy to have you appear from the past if he did. It was his plan to go to Flat Busted—Busted Heights!—and find out what had happened. If all was well, the discovery was to be a gift to you, a surprise."

Closing her eyes, Mrs. Watson whispered, "What did Julian change his name to?"

Fortune already knew the answer. Taking Jamie's letter from her pocket, she unfolded it and spread it on her lap. On the back of the second page, in the upper corner, in faded ink, was the original name of the man who had given the book it was torn from to Jamie. His father—Julian Beck.

CHAPTER EIGHTEEN

"I should have known," Mrs. Watson said mournfully to Fortune that night.

"How could you have?" asked Fortune gently. She was sitting on the edge of the bed, holding Mrs. Watson's hand, the two of them united by their loss, their shared grief.

Mrs. Watson closed her eyes. "A mother should know. I did know, in a way. He had Julian's eyes. And the first time he did 'To be or not to be' for us, it was as if it was Julian himself speaking the lines. But it was too impossible to believe. I thought he was dead."

They sat in silence for a while.

"Lola wants us to go back to Grass Valley with her," said Fortune at last.

Mrs. Watson nodded. "You're afraid to go, because you're hoping he'll come back, aren't you?"

"Aren't you?"

She sighed. "I know better, chicken. That damn male pride of his won't allow it. We can leave a message at the front desk. They'll tell him where we've gone. But the truth is, he can find us anytime he wants. There aren't many people more public than actors."

"Do you think we'll ever see him again?" asked Fortune, her voice quivering.

Mrs. Watson closed her eyes. "It's not likely. But if I've learned a single lesson from my years in the theater, it's that anything is possible."

The trip from Mad Jack's Gulch to Grass Valley took them through some of the most beautiful terrain they had ever seen. Yet Fortune and Mrs. Watson traveled through it as if they were blind.

"You're thinking about your young man, aren't you?" said Lola to Fortune late the second afternoon.

Fortune nodded.

"You must learn to forget him. Men! You cannot let yourself go to pieces over the loss of a man. I myself have loved many great men: the musician Liszt; the writer Dumas; even the king of Bavaria, who loved me back, but let me be exiled from his kingdom because he was weak. I have also had many husbands. Love comes, and it goes. I am sad, but I go on. It is the way of it for us, Fortune.

We are theater people. Theater people go on."

Theater people go on. How often had her father said that?

A few hours later they were actually in Grass Valley, riding along the planks that had been laid down to make the town's main street. "In San Francisco's streets the mud sometimes gets so deep they lose horses in it," said Lola contemptuously. "Here, we are more civilized."

Lola's house was fairly simple, a large white structure undistinguished from the ones around it except for the profusion of flowers, the fascinating cactus garden, and the grizzly bear cub in the backyard.

"Oh, Minerva!" cried Mrs. Watson when she first saw the bear. "Is that thing safe?"

"His teeth are no sharper than a critic's," said Lola simply, after which Mrs. Watson seemed perfectly at ease with the beast.

The bear was the largest creature in Lola's menagerie, but hardly the extent of it. In and around the house were also parrots, cats, dogs, a goat, and a lamb.

"Damnedest place I ever saw," muttered Mr. Patchett.

At first Fortune feared the others would be jealous over the way Lola was treating her. But they seemed to take it as her due, as the daughter of John and Laura Plunkett.

The day after their arrival Lola found them a house not too far from hers and, against Fortune's objections, paid the first month's rent.

"You will pay me back," said Lola, placing a finger over Fortune's lips. "Right now you need a home. Soon you must go on the road; you must begin to act again. You will tour the mining camps for a while, make some money, get some experience. Then come back here to spend the winter with Lola! Those things they call roads in this crazy country are bad then, and it is hard to travel."

Their days fell into an easy pattern now, as Lola made them welcome. She introduced the troupe to the players and artists who streamed through Grass Valley, coming to pay homage to her as if she were a patron saint. It was the strangest entourage Fortune had ever seen, a procession of the elegant and the scruffy, the great and the graceless, all of them with one thing in common: a love of the arts.

Among them were a poet Lola tended to encourage, and whom Fortune suspected of being more than slightly mad; an artist whose paintings of mining life were undeniably crude, yet seemed to blaze with an inner life of their own; and most intriguing of all, a strange little girl named Lotta Crabtree, who Lola was convinced was going to be a great star.

"Dance for Fortune," Lola would say to the child, and Lotta would go into one of the jigs or schottisches that Lola had taught her. She sang maudlin Irish songs with a haunting air that belied her age, as if she had actually suffered the heartbreak she sang of. And, like Lola herself, she exuded an irresistible spark of vitality that drew people to her.

"Lola's right, you know," said Mr. Patchett one day, standing beside Fortune and watching. "That child's going to be a star." Indeed, Fortune found she could hardly take her eyes off Lotta. Unpolished as she was, something about her was utterly compelling.

At night Lola would tell them stories of her past adventures, of her travels in India and Europe, and her great love for King Louis I of Bavaria. Sometimes she would act out portions of her favorite play, *Lola Montez in Bavaria,* an outrageous concoction based on her own life story.

Once she even demonstrated her famous Spider Dance, shaking large cork spiders from her voluminous skirts, then whirling about the room and stomping on them in a frenzy of terror. It was as bizarre a performance as anything

Fortune had ever seen, and though she was too much in awe of Lola to laugh herself, she understood how others might have, as the desk clerk in Mad Jack's Gulch had claimed.

In fact, it did not take Fortune long to learn the truth about Lola Montez. Her fame was based not on her ability as an actress, which was actually quite minimal, but on her great personality, which was astonishing. She drew people the way a flame draws moths, and divided them more sharply and significantly than a battle over religious doctrine.

The other thing Fortune learned from Lola was how good she was herself.

"Come, Fortune," Lola would say. "Let us try that scene from *Othello*. I want to see you do Desdemona." Then they would act out one of Lola's favorite scenes from the play.

Though Lola was hopeless, something in her knew how to bring out the best in Fortune. "No, no, no!" she would cry. "Not like that. Like *this!*" Then she would deliver the line in question in a way that was totally wrong, yet contained in it the exact hint Fortune needed to do it correctly.

It was a revelation for Fortune. She had thought her work in *Hamlet* opposite Jamie had been spectacular only because of the spark she caught from him. Now she knew that was not true. She was a fine actress. And she had it in her to be great.

That was small compensation for the loss of Jamie. Yet somehow it made her feel closer to him, for acting was all she had left of him, of his dreams. Her own brief dream of a life with him had been shattered. Believing that there could never be anyone else in the world for her, she clung to her craft as to a life raft. It was what kept her sane.

You'd be so proud, Papa, she'd think when she gave a particularly adept reading, or found a new way to express an emotion. *I wish you could see me.*

That thought did not bother her. She had accepted the loss of her father. It was the wish that Jamie could see what she was learning, how she was growing, that really gnawed at her.

At night she would take out his letter, crumpled and tear-stained from that first day, now lovingly preserved, and read it over before she went to sleep.

Come back! she would think sometimes as she sat in Lola's home and stared out at the wilderness. *Come back to the one who loves you.*

Then she would lift the chain that hung about her neck, and stare at the heart-shaped golden nugget that she always carried with her.

Walter, too, was grieving over the loss of Jamie. He was sure, somehow, that he was the cause of it—without ever knowing exactly what had happened. For Fortune and Mrs. Watson, in the way of women, had closed ranks. Jamie's letter, and the real reason he had left, had never been revealed to the men of the troupe. Even so, the big man would not look Fortune in the eye.

In mid-October Fortune and Mr. Patchett decided it was time to take the troupe on the road again. They packed their wagon, filling it with props, costumes, and sets they had made, or that Lola had given them, and headed for the mining camps.

"And a good thing it is we're going," said Mr. Patchett to her on the morning of their departure. "Aaron and Edmund were getting restless. Another day or so and they probably would have been getting into trouble."

As it was they were too busy for much trouble. They played a night or two in each town they came to, sometimes filling the house, when there was a house to fill (they were surprised at the number of towns that had real theaters), sometimes playing in the open, to a handful or a crowd—it didn't seem to matter as long as someone wanted to see their shows.

What Fortune both loved and hated was that many of the men came to the plays simply because she and Mrs. Watson were in them. The great shortage of women in the mining camps made

217

them shining attractions no matter how good (or bad) their plays were. It was nice to be the center of so much attention, but she would have preferred it if it had been for the quality of their art.

At every camp they came to Fortune asked about Jamie, at every performance searched the crowd for his familiar face.

It was never there.

She knew Mrs. Watson was watching the crowds as well. In their shared grief they had grown close in a way Fortune would never have thought possible even a month earlier. Often they spoke late into the night.

It was strange to realize that Mrs. Watson had once felt the same fears and longings that she experienced now, had had her own heart broken, perhaps even more deeply, by the loss of not only a husband but a child as well—a child she had now lost a second time.

One day there was a coldness in the air, and they knew without saying a word to one another that it was time to return to Grass Valley.

They passed the winter there in relative quiet, practicing new ideas, repairing costumes and sets, and dreaming of San Francisco. Word had come that a single concert ticket had recently been auctioned off for twelve hundred dollars there. And it was well known that, depending on how they liked the show, the audience was apt to throw anything from tomatoes and eggs to roses and gold dust.

Not that the troupe had done badly as it toured the mines. They had collected a tidy amount, much of it in the form of small pouches of gold dust thrown in enthusiastic response to the appearance of Fortune and Mrs. Watson.

Their old dream of building a theater was beginning to burn within them once more. They were once again close to that goal, no longer impoverished players but a prosperous troupe ready to head for San Francisco and theatrical gold.

And, of course, they listened to Lola as she told them story after story—how she had challenged an entire audience in Sacramento to a duel, crying, "Give me your pants and take my petticoats. You're not fit to be called men!" Or about her stormy love affair with the great composer Franz Liszt, or how she had been exiled by King Louis when he lost courage and gave in to the demands of the rabble.

And the world continued turning, and spring returned to gold country, and in time Plunkett's Players took to the road again, landing, eventually, in a place called Centipede Hollow, where they were to play out the final, tragic act of their westward journey.

CHAPTER NINETEEN

It had been raining for two days.

"I've got the peedoodles," said Mrs. Watson, wringing her hands.

Edmund stepped away from her. "Is it contagious?" he asked mockingly.

Mrs. Watson slapped at his arm. "No more than stupidity. It just means I'm nervous."

"Miner talk?" asked Fortune.

"Yes. I learned it from a wonderful man in Grass Valley. Anyway, this weather is making me anxious."

Fortune stifled a snort. Having listened to Mrs. Watson snore her way through prairie thunderstorms, she was not about to believe her friend was that upset by a little rain. She wondered what was really bothering her. Was she nervous because they would be doing their first performance of the season that night? Or was it that she was having a hard time taking her place as queen of the troupe once more?

Fortune smiled, feeling slightly wicked. One of her favorite amusements that winter had been watching Mrs. Watson try to cope with Lola. She seemed to swing from someplace between awe and admiration to complete and utter jealousy.

"There, there, my dear," said Walter, setting his hand, which was the size of a small frying pan, gently on Mrs. Watson's shoulder. "They'll love us. Just you wait and see."

The gesture only earned him a scowl and the tart response: "It's the weather!"

Fortune shook her head. Since the night of his gambling catastrophe, Walter had been trying desperately to redeem himself. Sometimes she wanted to grab him by the shoulders and shout, "Walter, I'm not mad anymore! Stop trying to make up for what you did, because you can't. No one can. Just be your sweet old self again and let it go at that."

Somehow she had never been able to bring herself to do it. And even if she had, it would not have set to rest the grudge Mrs. Watson now held against him for his part in Jamie's departure.

As Walter backed away, his eyes deep with hurt, Aaron and Mr. Patchett rejoined the group.

"Everything is ready," said Mr. Patchett,

rubbing his hands together. "It should be a good house. After being cooped up for the winter everyone is as restless as Hamlet's father. They're well ripe for a little imported entertainment."

"We're the first since fall?" asked Edmund.

Mr. Patchett shrugged. "Not everyone folded up their operations for the weather, so they've had a couple of troupes through here. But pickings have been slim, so they're glad to have another company in town. They've even heard of us—"

"Of course they have!" said Aaron. "We're famous throughout the West for burning down theaters and starting enormous brawls. People are dying to find out what we'll do tonight."

"I hope they won't be disappointed if we don't do anything more than give them a good show," said Fortune.

Aaron shrugged. "Who knows? These miners are all crazy." As he spoke, he gave her a private look that said, "Are you all right?"

Fortune smiled in response. Perhaps the only good thing that had come out of this dreary winter was that in the wake of Jamie's leaving she and Aaron had developed a real friendship.

Fortune had been astonished at how different things could be with a man once the love question was out of the way. She had never suspected that she could really be friends with Aaron. In fact, it had never really crossed her mind when she had thought that she loved him.

The idea had puzzled her. "Can you love someone without liking them?" she had asked Mrs. Watson one night when they were sitting in front of the fireplace in the cozy little home Lola had found for them.

Mrs. Watson had not answered the question right away, instead sat staring into the flames. "The problem with that question," she finally said, drawing her blanket around her, "is that it makes it sound like love should make sense. But it doesn't. Never has, never will. Loving and liking don't always have an awful lot to do with each other, at least not in my experience." She paused. "The tricky part of it is, while it's easy enough to fall in love with someone without liking them, you won't have much luck making it last that way. I loved Jamie's father with every fiber of my being, but the Lord alone knows what life would have been like if we had actually been able to live together."

"I see," said Fortune. "At least, I think I do."

"Your parents were wonderful that way," continued Mrs. Watson. "I don't believe I ever saw two people who liked each other more than those two."

"Didn't they love each other?" cried Fortune.

"Of course they did. Haven't you been listening to me? But they weren't just in love; they actually *liked* each other. Don't see that too much these days. Take Lola. I never could keep track of how many husbands she had."

"Three," said Fortune. "I think."

Mrs. Watson nodded. "She probably loved every one of them, too. But I doubt she liked 'em much."

Though Fortune had chuckled at the observation, it stayed with her. As she studied Aaron now, she wished that they could have been friends earlier. *My fault, I guess. I was so wrapped up in trying to get him to love me I never really thought about being his friend.* She was pretty certain the interest he had shown in her last summer was due more to childlike jealousy, a fear of losing something he had been able to take for granted, than to any real feeling of love for her. Once Jamie had left, Aaron's interest seemed to dwindle, too.

Of course, it could be that he realizes there is no one else in the world for me now, she thought occasionally. She wanted to believe he was sensitive enough to see that.

Whatever it was, she was enjoying his friendship; it had helped her through some of the worst days of the winter.

Not the truly worst ones, she reminded herself. Those were the days when it stormed, and she spent from dawn till dusk sitting at the window, staring out and wondering if Jamie was all right, if he was sheltered, safe—or if he was alone, lost in the raging weather, with no one to care for him.

Sometimes she sat that way for hours, tears running slowly and steadily down her face. It was stupid, she knew, but she couldn't help it.

Other times she had felt a sudden surge of fierce anger at Jamie for not trusting her more, for not trying to find out what had really happened that night.

Walter came upon her once when she was in her sorrow. His face had crumpled in despair and self-loathing, and he had disappeared into his room for three days. He said he was too sick to come down to meals. In her heart Fortune knew his only disease was shame.

But that's past! she told herself firmly. *We're on the road again, we perform tonight, it's just like the old days . . . except . . . except . . .*

She turned and ran from the group, so no one would see her tears.

"You all right?" asked a gentle voice a few moments later.

She turned and let Aaron hold her while she wept.

"Hope they don't run too late," said one of the men in the front row. "The rain's been gettin' worse all day. Looks like we might have a real gullywasher tonight."

Wonderful, thought Fortune, listening in the wings. *No one's going to pay attention to the show because they'll be worrying about the weather.*

What was worse, she knew she would be worrying about the weather, too. They had a performance scheduled in the next town up the line tomorrow; if the weather was too bad they might not make it.

But once the show began she didn't worry about the weather. She was swept away by being on stage again, being in front of an audience that responded to what they did, cared what happened to the people they were pretending to be. With a jolt of surprise, she realized how much she had missed making people laugh, making them cry. And, being honest with herself, she admitted the addiction she had tried for years to deny. She had missed the applause!

The next morning it was still raining, a gentle drizzle that didn't prevent travel, simply made everything wet and uncomfortable. Complaining heartily, they packed the wagon, harnessed the horses, and headed south. Everyone except Aaron, who had to drive, sat in back to stay out of the rain.

The road was preposterous, a slick trail of mud that sucked at the wagon wheels, clung to the horses' hooves, and seemed to actively try to keep them from moving at all.

"Maybe we should turn back," said Mrs. Watson. The wagon cover was beginning to leak, and a rivulet of water was running along the spot where she usually sat.

"I don't want to miss a playing date if we can help it," said Fortune, speaking loudly to be heard above the drum of the rain. "It's not professional."

"Fortune, you'd better come up here," called Aaron.

Leaving Mrs. Watson to stew, Fortune scrambled up beside Aaron. The rain was coming down harder now, and almost instantly her clothes were soaked through and clinging to her skin.

"Look," said Aaron.

Ahead lay a stream, swollen over its banks, the water a churning mass of brown.

"Can we make it across?"

"I don't know. That's why I called you up here. I'm a little nervous about it. I'll try if you want.

Most of the other streams we've come to out here weren't very deep."

She turned back to the others and made a choice. "Edmund—I need you to go ahead of us and see how deep that stream runs."

"Are you crazy?" he replied, his voice surly.

"Afraid you'll get wet?" she asked, trying to jolly him a bit.

For an uncomfortable moment they stared at each other. Fortune wanted desperately to turn away, but telling herself that Lola would never let a mere man stare her down, she decided that neither would she. And even though her stomach seemed to be churning as rapidly as the water beneath them, her gaze never faltered.

After what seemed like an eternity Edmund looked at his shirt, which was already clinging to his skin, and laughed. He climbed out of the back of the wagon and headed around it to the stream. By the time he was halfway across, the water was still no deeper than his knees.

"Looks safe," said Aaron, shaking the reins and urging the horses forward.

"Wait!" said Fortune. "He might not have reached the main bed yet."

But in another moment Edmund was standing on the far bank. He turned and waved them on.

A rumble of thunder shuddered through the

sky. Aaron shook the reins. "Gee, Romeo. Haw, Juliet. Let's roll!"

They splashed into the water. As if on signal, the skies chose that moment to unleash their load. What had started as a drizzle and gradually turned to a moderate rain became, suddenly and instantly, a torrential downpour.

"I can't see!" cried Aaron.

Fortune grabbed his arm. The rain was so heavy it felt as if they had actually fallen into the water. From behind her she heard an angry voice yelling, "Oh, Minerva! I should have been born a duck!"

The horses whinnied in fright, and when a jagged streak of lightning slashed down nearby, Romeo—his eyes rolling in terror—lifted his hooves and pawed at the air.

Aaron slashed at the gelding's rump with the reins. At the same time he yelled to Fortune, "I don't know what to do! I can't see to get across and I can't back them up."

"Then stay here."

"We can't do that!"

"Why not?" she asked, surprised by the urgency in his voice.

"This streambed could flood fast if this keeps up! The water washes off the hills and—"

He was interrupted by Walter poking his head

up from behind them. "I'll lead the team across!" he shouted. "I think it's the safest way."

Fortune could feel Aaron's relief. "Watch your footing," he called. But Walter was gone already, making his way back through the wagon to go out through the rear.

Fortune had expected the intensity of the downpour to diminish after a short time. To her amazement it continued unabated, as if the air itself had turned to water.

She realized that every muscle in her body was knotted like a cord and told herself to relax. Aaron knew what he was doing; worrying wasn't going to help.

Her body refused to obey the command. She tasted blood and realized she had bit her lip until it was bleeding.

Walter went splashing past them, and a moment later the wagon began rolling forward.

Aaron cursed.

"What is it?" asked Fortune.

"The water is getting higher already. Look!"

Leaning over the edge of the wagon, she could actually see the frothing stream creeping up on the wheels. Without intending to, she gasped. "We've got to get across fast!"

"We can't go any faster than Walter can lead us," said Aaron. "Damn!" he added, in response to a lurch of the wagon.

"What is going on?" demanded Mrs. Watson, appearing behind them.

Before Fortune could answer, she found herself clutching Aaron's arm for support as the right front wheel lifted over a little hump and fell into a hole. The wagon jerked to a stop, listing dangerously to the side.

"Damn," said Aaron again. He threw down the reins and leaped over the side. Fortune scrambled down after him.

"Fortune Plunkett, you come back here!" cried Mrs. Watson. "I promised your father I'd take care of you. I—"

Her words were lost in the storm. Fortune slogged through the stream, hardly able to tell where the water left off and the air began. The lightning was more frequent now. Juliet, always nervous in a storm, was whinnying and kicking. Mr. Patchett, who had come around from the back of the wagon, was standing with Aaron. They were both studying the wheel.

"How bad is it?" she asked, stepping between them.

"I don't know," said Aaron. "I wish Jamie was here. He always knew what to do in this kind of situation."

"We've got that long wooden bar he insisted we

buy back in Independence. It's one of the few things that didn't fall out on the mountain that day. He said it was to pry up the wagon if we got stuck."

"I'll get it!" said Mr. Patchett. As he began splashing back toward the wagon, Fortune realized the water was halfway up his long legs.

"I'll go get Edmund," she said. "We're going to need all the help we can get."

"Be careful!" roared Aaron, shouting against the storm.

Fortune started off, using the horses as a guide. *I can't even see the other side,* she thought in panic. *How will I get there?* Her panic flared even higher when she bumped into a dark shape in the rain and it reached out and grabbed her.

"Fortune! What are you doing?"

It was Walter. She had forgotten that he had gone ahead to lead the team across.

"I'm going to get Edmund," she told him. "We need him back there."

"I'll go. You stay here and keep the horses calm. You're better with them than I am anyway."

Fortune started to object, then decided he was right. She watched fondly as the giant waded toward the far bank, knowing that he was still trying to make up for the night that he had lost all their money.

Suddenly Romeo threw back his head,

trumpeting in terror. The movement pulled her off her feet, and it was only her grip on the harness that kept her from being swept away by the current. She tried frantically to calm him again.

It seemed an eternity before Walter returned with Edmund. The water, rising steadily, was midway up Fortune's thigh when she heard Edmund's angry voice sputtering about fools who couldn't drive.

Shut up, she thought. *Just shut up and help.*

Then suddenly it didn't make any difference whether Edmund helped or not. The rain tapered off as quickly as it had begun.

Fortune almost collapsed with relief.

Mr. Patchett smiled. "Well, well—that feels as good as remembering a line that you thought you had lost."

The moment of relief was broken by a piercing scream from Mrs. Watson.

Snapping around, Fortune saw a wall of water roaring toward them. It was far up the creek bed, but rolling forward at an appalling rate.

"The horses!" she cried. "Help me free the horses."

Walter was at her side at once. Her fingers, chilled by the rain, felt as if they were made of lead. The straps, resisting her fumbling efforts to loose them, seemed to have taken on a malevolent intelligence of their own. Fortune thought she was going to scream in frustration. Glancing back, she could see the water getting closer. Mrs. Watson had surrendered to hysterics.

"Edmund!" cried Fortune. "Get her to shore. Hurry!"

She turned her attention back to Juliet's harness. "Come on!" she urged the stubborn leather. "Loosen up!"

But the moisture had caused it to swell so much that it seemed hopelessly jammed.

"Got it!" cried Walter, freeing Romeo. He slapped the gelding's rump. "Go on, boy! Get to shore!"

He hurried to where Fortune stood fumbling with one of the stubborn straps. Behind her she could hear Aaron and Mr. Patchett trying to free the wagon wheel from the hole.

"Enough!" cried Mr. Patchett. "Head for the bank!"

"I can't leave Juliet!" cried Fortune.

Before she could say another word, the water was upon them. It struck her like a falling tree, sweeping her feet off the river bottom. She clung desperately to Juliet, but the horse staggered and fell, too. The wagon went over. Fortune could hear the wood cracking and splintering.

I've got to get this undone or Juliet will drown!

The fear seemed to give her a strength she had never known before. With one last burst of effort she managed to undo the harness.

Juliet thrashed desperately, trying to get to her feet. Fortune clung to the horse's neck.

Together, they were swept away by the flood.

CHAPTER TWENTY

Fortune clung to Juliet's neck, trying desperately to keep her own head above the rushing water. Yet it seemed that no sooner would she break the surface, gasping for air, than the water would close over her again. It was as if she were in the grasp of some great and powerful god who was picking her up and tossing her down at his whim. She fought in vain against the merciless rush of the current, the tangling of her sodden clothes, the desperate need for air.

Juliet's terrified whinnying rang in Fortune's ears as she thrashed against the freezing brown water that swirled around her.

Her struggles were nothing in the face of the flood's power. A sense of crushing helplessness overwhelmed her. She was sure she was going to die until suddenly . . . there was hope.

As she pieced it together afterward, what saved

236

her was that Walter had clung to the harness traces when the flood swept over them. Rather than fighting the water, he had let it carry him away—perhaps because, unlike Fortune, he had nothing solid to hang on to. That had changed when the current thrust him against a tree standing in the flood path. With great effort the giant had managed to get himself on the far side of it. Struggling to keep his head above water, he wrapped the leather strap around the trunk.

That was all the help Juliet needed. When the harness caught, there was a wrenching jolt. Then the mare braced herself against it. For a long time her hooves were unable to find sure footing. But by bracing against the strap she was able to lunge up out of the water so that she—and Fortune— could breathe.

Fortune had struggled desperately to hold on and keep her head above water as much as possible. Long after she would wake in the night, remembering again the muddy smell of the flood, the force of it against her body, the fierce chill of it on her skin, the roar as it surged past her.

And then, as rapidly as it had struck, the worst of the current had passed by. They would learn later that what had caught them had been more than just a foothills flash flood. A few weeks earlier two miners attempting to get at more gold had temporarily diverted part of the stream from its normal bed. The heavy rains and rapidly rising water had broken their dam, and it was the freeing of that pent-up water that nearly cost the troupe their lives.

She hadn't known that at the time though. She simply knew she was wildly grateful when the dreadful pounding stopped and Juliet was able to stagger to her feet.

Then she saw Walter's body, dangling from the lowest branches of the tree. She began to scream, convinced that he was dead. At the same time Mr. Patchett, Edmund, and Aaron—who had been pounding along the bank, trying to keep up—came splashing through the water toward them. Edmund grabbed Juliet and led her to safety. Then he splashed back out into the stream, because though Mr. Patchett had freed Walter from the tree, it took Edmund's strength as well to drag the big man back to the bank.

Fortune saw them struggling with Walter's body as Aaron was lifting her from the water. After that she collapsed and became unconscious.

An hour or so later, when she awoke, the first thing she did was reach into her dress for Jamie's letter, which she had carried with her throughout the winter.

It was nothing but a sodden mass of ink-stained paper.

Tears welled up in her eyes. She had read the letter every night before she went to sleep. Now it was gone, and she mourned its loss even more than the loss of their faithful old wagon, which had been shattered by the flood.

At least she still had the nugget.

They decided to backtrack to Centipede Hollow. Though they had left it by only a few miles, it was morning by the time the weary band staggered back to the top of the last hill that overlooked the town.

When they looked down on the place, saw the desolation, Fortune heard a small groan. It was a moment before she realized that it had come from her own lips. After yesterday's disaster, the catastrophe below seemed too much to bear.

Water covered every street in the town, as if the place had been built in a lake to begin with. Here and there could be seen the remains of a building that had been put up too rapidly, or with a shoddy foundation, and was now nothing but a heap of rubble. The hill on the other side of the main street was dotted with tents and makeshift shelters.

The sight drew a collective moan from the

group. They had managed to get through the last twenty-four hours partly on the belief that they would find food and shelter when they finally made it back here. They hadn't been expecting to find yet another disaster area.

Still, bad as the situation was, at least they could find some kind of help.

Besides, there was nowhere else to go.

Fortune knew she should probably be concerned about the townspeople and what they had suffered. But when she groaned, she had been thinking only of her stomach. Wearily, the five who were still on their feet trudged down the hill. Aaron was leading Romeo. Walter, semiconscious, half delirious and gibbering about Hamlet's ghost, was slung over the horse's broad back.

Fortune dropped back to examine him. Walking beside Romeo, she put her hand on Walter's shoulder and whispered, "I'd be dead now if it wasn't for you, old friend." She wondered if he could even hear her. "Oh, Walter, do you feel like you've redeemed yourself yet? I stopped being angry long ago. Don't leave us. Not now. *Please!*"

She shook her head, fighting back the tears, then whispered again, "Please!"

The mere act of walking through Centipede

Hollow was a major effort, since water still stood in all but the highest spots, and where there wasn't water there was mud—clinging, catching, holding mud.

Fortune had been hoping that they would find a doctor when they got back to the town. But though there was urgent need of one, since broken bones and fever were everywhere, no medical man had settled here.

"I wish we were home, back where it's civilized!" said Fortune angrily. She was speaking to Edmund and Aaron. The three of them had spent hours combing the town for someone to help Walter. At one point, her nerves frayed beyond endurance, Fortune had found herself standing in the middle of a street, screaming at the mud to let her loose. When she had finally realized how stupid she must look, she had glanced around, then begun working quietly to free herself.

They were standing now in the lobby of the hotel where she had browbeaten the clerk into letting them have a room on credit because their money, along with their props and their clothing, had been lost with the wagon.

Actually, she would gladly have parted with all of it to have Walter recover. They had lost everything before, and regained it. The only thing that had disappeared in the flood that couldn't be replaced was her letter from Jamie.

Wearily, the three dragged themselves to their room, where they found Mr. Patchett and Mrs. Watson, seemingly numb beyond response, sitting beside Walter's cot, silent and staring.

Two days later they were sitting down to breakfast when Edmund suddenly bolted from the table. Fortune hesitated, then ran after him to see if he was all right.

She found him kneeling in the street outside the hotel, vomiting. Her stomach churned at the smell.

When he was done, she helped him to his feet, holding her breath against the odor.

That was the first sign they had of what others in town had already discovered during the night. The cholera had arrived, as it so often did in towns that had suffered a flood.

Poor Edmund's supercilious elegance failed him utterly as the disease took over his body, racking him with fever, causing him to spew out liquids violently.

Mrs. Watson was next to fall. The disease devastated her. It wasn't the thought of dying—it was the simple betrayal by her body, the humiliation of losing control of her functions. Fortune's heart ached for Mrs. Watson when she heard her sobbing in her bed.

Walter and Aaron followed in rapid succession. Because of Walter's weakened condition, the disease seemed to strike him hardest of all.

Only Fortune and Mr. Patchett remained untouched.

Fortune now found herself cast in a role she had never expected to play: nurse to the sick and the dying.

Few residents of Centipede Hollow escaped the touch of the disease. Of those who did, many fled, their terror of contracting the scourge outweighing any compassion they might feel for those who had already been stricken by it.

Fortune longed to flee, too. Centipede Hollow had become one vast sickroom, and it brought to mind all too painfully the memories of her parents' last hours.

Shame-faced, Mr. Patchett suggested it to her.

"Maybe we should go," he said late one afternoon. "There's too much death here."

Fortune nodded. She had seen too much death, and it was weighing heavily on her.

But as she started to pack her bags, something stopped her. In her mind, she imagined Jamie being struck down by the cholera, too, and wondered if anyone would nurse him if that should happen.

She went back to where Mr. Patchett was waiting for her.

"We're staying," she said.

He looked at her for a moment, then shrugged.

Rolling up their sleeves, they walked among the dead and dying, and did what had to be done.

CHAPTER TWENTY-ONE

To her amazement, Fortune found the work of nursing the sick very rewarding. Though she was exhausted, terrified, revolted by the filth and the suffering, when she entered a room and the moaning creature that lay on a cot saw her and, for a moment, seemed to be free of the fear and the pain, she felt something she had never experienced before, something that struck deeper even than the applause she had learned to love.

In a matter of days she had become the stuff of legend. The miners referred to her as "The Angel of Centipede Hollow," and many a miner would claim in later years that he survived the cholera because he lay in his bed day after day "waiting for his Fortune," unwilling to die until he had had his chance to see her that day, and too filled with hope to die once he had.

Fortune herself never fully realized the impact

she had on those men. Traveling the streets in an old blue cloak that one of the other women had given her to wear, she would come in from the fog or the darkness, her golden hair tumbling over her shoulders, her eyes filled with compassion, and suddenly make life seem worthwhile again.

Her world became an endless round of the sick and the dying, a sea of mud, an overwhelming stench of disease and filth that could not be escaped no matter where she went.

Yet she would have been content, were it not for her fears for her friends. Edmund, with remarkable strength, had thrown off the disease in less than three days. Weak but willing, he joined the nursing effort by helping with the preparation of food for the victims.

Fortune, astonished, said nothing.

Jamie was on her mind constantly during these days. Every time she ministered to a sick miner, wiped someone's brow, or fed him broth, she wondered if Jamie was well, and if he was not if anyone was caring for him.

She wondered, too, what he thought of her, if he ever thought of her at all.

Sometimes she wondered if he was even alive. That thought, when it came, was ruthlessly purged. She would lift the chain that hung about her neck, cup the golden nugget in her palm, and try to keep from weeping. Even when not holding it she was aware of the heart-shaped nugget where it rested against her own heart.

She tried to console herself with the knowledge that Plunkett's Players had been lucky. By rights, more of them should have lost the battle with cholera. But Edmund was almost fully recovered, and Aaron and Mrs. Watson were both doing well. The troupe had beaten the odds. Yet she was greedy. She wanted *all* of them to survive.

And it seemed clear that Walter would not.

Sometimes at night, when she simply could not walk another step, Fortune would take out the banjo a dying miner had given her, and sing quietly to herself, the little songs she had been writing about California.

If she sat on the porch of the hotel when she did this, miners would soon gather about her, in the same way the wagon people had. Then she would feel once more what it meant to be a performer.

She understood, in those days, how her songs could be as important as the nursing she was doing, for she could see the gratitude in the eyes of the men who listened—gratitude for what her songs gave them: a momentary release from the sorrow that surrounded them, and an escape valve for pent-up emotions. When she sang of homes that were far away, she could count on bringing them to tears every time.

It gave her a sense of power, and a sense of responsibility.

Late one night Fortune sat on the porch, strumming the banjo and thinking about all that had happened in the single year since their wagon had rolled into Busted Heights the previous April.

A heavy fog closed over the streets, so that the dim glow of yellow from the window behind her provided the only illumination.

Suddenly she began to weep. Seven more men had died that day, despite everything she had done. It was no surprise. Everyone knew what the odds were. But she could never get used to it. She wanted to be back on the stage, where death was a bit of pretending, and at the end of the show everyone came back to take a bow.

Sorrow found voice in song. Plucking the banjo, she began to sing the words she had written while they were on the trail:

> *"When I rise up*
> *And look around,*
> *My home I cannot see . . ."*

She stopped, the painful hurt in her throat too thick to let the words pass. But from out of the mist and the darkness a sweetly familiar tenor voice picked up the lyric, finished the verse.

> *"For I have wandered*
> *Far away . . .*
> *What will become of me?"*

She seemed to hang suspended in space, unable to speak, to move, to breath. From the corner of her eye she saw a movement in the fog at the end of the porch. It freed her to move again. Silently she placed the banjo at her side. Then she stood and brushed out her skirt.

"I'm here," she said softly.

The mist seemed to cling to the man who stepped forward, hiding his face. It made no difference; she knew who it was.

She wanted to run to him, throw her arms around him, cover him with kisses.

But she couldn't. Not yet. Not until she knew how he felt about her.

He stepped still closer. She was on fire with the need to reach out to him. But she had to wait, had to know if he would accept her, forgive her. . . .

Still not saying a word, Jamie stepped out of the mist. His eyes were dark, as if he had not slept in a long time, and they seemed deeper than ever, full of wonder.

Slowly, almost fearfully, he reached out to touch her hair.

A sob broke from his chest. "My God. You are here. And you're alive!"

Trembling, she placed her hand over his.

"I've kept track of you every day since I left," he whispered. "When I learned about the flood, the cholera, heard what you were doing here, I had to come. Even if you didn't want me, I had to see if you were all right, to see if . . . if you needed me."

The words caught in his throat. They were unnecessary. She saw everything she needed in his eyes.

Tentatively, still trembling, but knowing that he was willing to risk even the horror of cholera on her behalf, she reached out her hand and laid it on his chest.

"Jamie." Her body shook like a leaf in the wind, and no more words would come. It didn't matter. His arms were around her now, and he was holding her against him so tightly it felt as if they were a single being.

"Oh, Fortune," he gasped. "Oh, God, you don't know how I've missed you. Every day was a little death, every night an eternity in hell. There hasn't been a morning I've woken without you on my mind, a night when you weren't the last thing I thought of before I went to sleep."

"I thought I would die when you went away,"

she whispered. She drew away from him slightly, remembering how he had been hurt by what he saw. "Let me tell you what happened."

He covered her lips, first with his finger, then with a kiss. "It doesn't matter," he said a few moments later. "I don't care what happened, as long as you love me now."

"I do." She pulled his face back down to hers. "I do."

After a time she took Jamie into the hotel and led him to Walter's bedside. He gasped, and Fortune realized again how old and shrunken their friend now looked.

Jamie turned at her, and she could read the question in his eyes: *Is he going to make it?*

She shook her head.

Before either of them could speak, Walter opened his eyes.

"Jamie?" he asked, struggling to lift his head. Then, when he was sure of what he was seeing, he held out his hand. "Jamie! Do you know me?"

"'Excellent well,'" said Jamie, reaching down to take Walter's hand. "'You are a fishmonger.'"

"It is you!" said Walter, clutching him desperately. "You came back!"

"Couldn't stay away!"

"I've been waiting for you." He gasped, and

broke into a fit of coughing. When it finally subsided, he said, "There's something you have to see!"

He turned to Fortune. "Show him." He reached up and touched her neck, laying his fingers lightly over the chain she had worn throughout the winter. "Show him what you always have with you. . . ."

Without a word, Fortune drew out the heart-shaped nugget.

"See!" Walter was smiling now, his face more peaceful than she had seen it in months. "See, Jamie, I didn't waste *all* your gold."

Jamie looked startled. "What do you mean?"

"Later," whispered Fortune. "I'll tell you later."

Walter took Jamie's hand and squeezed it fiercely. "Be good to her, boy," he whispered. "Be good to her. If you don't, I'll come back. I'll haunt you fiercer than the ghost of Hamlet's father."

He leaned back and closed his eyes. "I always wanted to get the death scene," he whispered. His hand tightened on Jamie's. His massive body, shrunken and wasted by the disease, twitched in a final spasm. And then he was gone.

Jamie stood without moving for a long time. Finally he released Walter's hand and placed it tenderly on the old man's chest.

Moving slowly, as if with a great weariness, Fortune pulled the other limp hand on top of it. Then, repeating a gesture she had made all too many times in the last few days, she drew the sheet over his still and silent face.

After a time she took Jamie's hand, warm and pulsing with life, and led him from the room.

"Tell me what happened," he said urgently, as if life would always be too short. "Tell me every-thing—everything you've done and thought and heard and seen. And then I'll tell you about me—about how much I love you, and about the million letters I wrote and tore up, and how you were on my mind every minute of every hour, and about the fortune in gold I've dug out of the hills, and—"

"It can wait," said Fortune, tracing the line of his jaw with her fingertip. "I've got everything I need right here."

He took her in his arms and made everything else disappear.

Three weeks later, on a morning brilliant with sunshine, the six members of Plunkett's Players crested a California hill.

"There it is!" whooped Mr. Patchett, who was walking alongside the new wagon they had bought with the money Jamie had dug from the hills. "There . . . it . . . is!"

"The promised land," said Aaron, who was walk-ing beside him. His voice held no trace of cynicism.

Fortune felt her heart leap. *It really is beautiful,* she thought, gazing down at the city her father had set out to reach over two years before. The sparkling waters of the broad bay where the city lay waiting seemed to beckon them on. Gulls wheeled and cried above great ships with furled sails that sat rocking at anchor. To the west the blue-gray waters of the Pacific stretched as far as the eye could see, until they were lost in the haze of the horizon.

Papa! Oh, I wish you could see it. I wish you could be here with us.

"Ready, Mrs. Halleck?" asked Jamie softly.

Fortune reached out and took her husband's hand. "Give me just a minute longer, Mr. Halleck. I never really expected this to happen."

He smiled and in the moment of astonishing warmth that flooded her heart she thought, *This is it. This is home. It's with him, wherever that might be.*

She smiled. "I'm ready now."

With a smile as big as tomorrow he looked over his shoulder, into the wagon, and said, "Ready . . . Mom?"

"As ready as I'll ever be, my chicks," replied Mrs. Watson happily.

Jamie shook the reins. Romeo and Juliet started forward.

Fortune took out her new guitar and began to sing.

Behind them was the land they had chal-lenged and survived.

Around them, on foot or in the wagon, were four dear, dear friends.

And just ahead—there at last—lay San Francisco, and all their golden dreams.

About the Author

Bruce Coville is one of today's best-loved authors, with over ten million books in print. *Fortune's Journey* grew out of his love for the theater, especially his writing and directing plays for and with young people. "I wanted to be able to share some of the terrific energy and excitement that occurs when young people do theater," he says, "and this seemed the most natural way for me to do it." Bruce Coville lives in Syracuse, New York.